"Since when are yo...
personal life?"

"Touché." David took Mia's hand, slowly rubbed her palm with his thumb.

She tensed, but in a good way. This was David touching her, his face so close that she could see the light flecks of amber in his brown eyes. Funny, she'd always thought they were much darker, more serious.

She straightened, tried to ignore the disturbing sensations his thumb caused. "In fact, Mr. Pearson, you really don't know anything about me, do you?"

His gaze touched her mouth, lingered, and then leisurely moved up to her eyes. "Don't I?"

He wrapped his fingers around her hand and tugged her closer. "My intentions must be fairly obvious now," he said in a low voice. Then he put his mouth on hers, his lips soft and supple.

David knew how to kiss; he was even better than she'd imagined. When he retreated, lingering long enough to touch his lips to hers one last time, she nearly whimpered in protest.

"I've wanted to do that for three years..."

Blaze

Dear Reader,

Second Time Lucky is the first book in my Spring Break series. What a fun series this has been for me to write. The stories take place in Hawaii, where I was born, raised. I spent my childhood years on the windward side of Oahu—Kailua to be exact—and then moved to Maui shortly after I graduated from the University of Hawaii.

A few years later, I married a mainlander who transferred often with his job, and I moved away from the islands. Although I return often to visit family, I don't get around Oahu much anymore. So when I sat down to write Mia and David's story, I found myself revisiting places I hadn't been in years. I had to imagine myself as a tourist, just like my hero and heroine, seeing the island's natural beauty as if it were the first time. Writing these stories has been like a blast from the past, my own little Spring Break. And I hope these books inspire you to think about experiencing a little Hawaiian magic yourself.

Happy reading!

Debbi Rawlins

Debbi Rawlins

SECOND TIME LUCKY

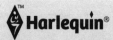

TORONTO NEW YORK LONDON
AMSTERDAM PARIS SYDNEY HAMBURG
STOCKHOLM ATHENS TOKYO MILAN MADRID
PRAGUE WARSAW BUDAPEST AUCKLAND

Recycling programs
for this product may
not exist in your area.

ISBN-13: 978-0-373-79607-6

SECOND TIME LUCKY

Printed in U.S.A.

ABOUT THE AUTHOR

Debbi Rawlins lives in central Utah, out in the country, surrounded by woods and deer and wild turkeys. It's quite a change for a city girl, who didn't even know where the state of Utah was until four years ago. Of course, unfamiliarity has never stopped her. Between her junior and senior years of college she spontaneously left her home in Hawaii and bummed around Europe for five weeks by herself. And much to her parents' delight, returned home with only a quarter in her wallet.

Books by Debbi Rawlins

This is for all the working moms
who need a spring break more than anyone.
Women with dogs and cats totally count.

Prologue

SHE WASN'T THERE. Disappointed, Mia Butterfield shaded her eyes against the bright sun and scanned the crowded park, her gaze quickly skipping over the noontime joggers and past the rows of nannies, whose concentration was split between children and gossip. With it being unseasonably warm for January, she'd felt certain Annabelle would be here walking her dog, or rather being walked by the oversize part St. Bernard and part Rottweiler she'd affectionately named Mr. Muffin.

Barely five feet tall and close to eighty, Mia's new friend should have had a nice little Yorkie or toy poodle as a companion, but no, not Annabelle. She preferred the big moose of a mutt that she'd found at the local shelter. Mia had only met Annabelle Albright six weeks ago when Mr. Muffin had spied a rabbit and pulled away from the older woman. Mia had been walking back from the courthouse to her office when she encountered the runaway dog. He'd literally run into her, costing her a pair of forty-dollar pantyhose and the three-inch heel of her new Jimmy Choos.

The upside was that Mia had made a new friend that

day. A much-needed friend. Her two best buds lived thousands of miles away, but the truth was, Annabelle served a need neither of Mia's college friends could. The woman had an unbiased ear. She listened, her gaze clear, her smile knowing, her rare questions about clarity, not judgment. Sometimes the silence frustrated Mia. Here she was twenty-eight and all she wanted was someone to tell her what to do. She hated that streak of vulnerability.

From the time she was a kid she'd always been a take-charge person, fully in control, absolutely clear on what she wanted. Her younger brother and sister had come to her for advice, as had her friends. When she'd graduated from law school with honors, no one had been surprised. Not even when she'd been recruited by one of the most prestigious law firms in Manhattan. She hadn't bothered explaining to her family what an incredible opportunity that was for a young lawyer.

In retrospect, it was a good thing she hadn't made a big deal of it because then for sure they wouldn't understand why she wanted to quit. All of it. Just walk away. Start fresh. No, they wouldn't get it. She barely did herself.

The mere thought of what she wanted to do twisted her stomach into knots. She stared down at the white paper bag in her hand and sighed. She didn't care about the apples and yogurt she'd bought at the corner bodega. The main reason she'd taken a lunch break was in the hope of seeing Annabelle.

"Mia!"

At the sound of the familiar voice, she turned around to see Annabelle being dragged toward her by the big dog. Prepared for an onslaught of large paws and sloppy kisses, Mia knew better than to crouch.

"Hey, Mr. Muffin." She held out a firm hand for him to sniff. His attention immediately switched to the paper bag. "Seriously, I don't think you'd be that interested."

"If it's food, he's interested," Annabelle said with a throaty laugh, her remarkably unlined face artfully made up. "Come on, Mr. Muffin, don't be a mooch." She tugged on the leash to get his attention, and with her other hand reached into the pocket of a smartly tailored burgundy jacket that had once been elegantly in style. "Here you go, you big lug." She produced a plastic bag of treats and made him sit before passing him a MilkBone.

"I was hoping I'd see you here today." Mia straightened, anxious to take advantage of the dog's temporary distraction.

"It's marvelous weather. Can you believe it's January?"

"I know. I can't afford the break but I couldn't help myself."

Annabelle waved a gloved hand. "You work too hard as it is." She saw that the dog had finished and quickly gave him another MilkBone. "He shouldn't have so many treats," she said absently, looking over her shoulder. "Where is that young man?"

"Young man?"

"Oh, there he is. Good." Annabelle signaled to a blond teenage boy on a skateboard near the fork in the sidewalk.

He zoomed toward them, skillfully avoiding a strolling couple before pulling to a stop in front of Annabelle. "Hey, Mrs. Albright. I'm not late, am I?"

"Right on time." She handed him the leash. "A half

an hour should tire him out." She crouched to nuzzle the dog's bulky neck, her fluid movement that of a much younger woman, a tribute to her early Broadway days. "Isn't that right, Mr. Muffin? You be a good boy, you hear?"

With hopeful eyes, the dog watched her pass the treats to the teenager, and then happily trotted off alongside the boy. Annabelle continued to watch the pair disappear while Mia found a bench partially shaded by a bare but huge old elm.

"Who's the boy?" Mia asked, as she brushed off the bench seat.

"Kevin, my neighbor's son." Annabelle joined her. "But you'll walk Mr. Muffin while I'm away on my trip?"

"What trip? You didn't tell me you were going anywhere."

"Oh, it's this cruise." Annabelle waved a dismissive hand, looking less than thrilled. "I'd promised a friend a few months back."

"Good for you." Mia rubbed her friend's arm. "It'll be great to get out of the city. Where are you going?"

"I don't actually know. Hamilton—" She cleared her throat. "—my friend, is in charge of all that."

Mia hid a smile. So, Annabelle had a gentleman friend who wanted to sweep her away. Which was made all the sweeter since Mia doubted the woman could afford a vacation of any sort otherwise.

Mia opened her bag and gave Annabelle an apple.

"Thank you, dear." The woman smiled. "You never forget that Granny Smith is my favorite. But I already ate my lunch."

Mia shrugged. "Save it for later. I bought yogurt, too."

Annabelle searched Mia's face, making Mia avert

her gaze in case her intentions were too obvious. She guessed the woman was struggling financially, but was too proud to accept charity. Her clothes and shoes were well made and had probably cost a few bucks new, but most of her wardrobe should have been donated years ago. Still, she was always impeccably groomed, her white hair and makeup tended with great care, even her short buffed fingernails were nicely maintained. She clearly took pride in her appearance and even greater pride in remaining self-sufficient. Mia had made the mistake of offering to help buy food and hiring a dog walker for Mr. Muffin, and was abruptly shot down.

"So, tell me what's on your mind," Annabelle said with her usual forthrightness.

Mia hesitated. "I hate my job." There, she'd said it out loud. "I do," she insisted when Annabelle twisted around to narrow her faded blue eyes on Mia.

"What brought this on?"

"The hours are long. I have no social life." She shrugged helplessly. "It's sort of a combination of things."

Annabelle's expression softened. "Are you thinking about changing firms?"

A sudden chill breeze made Mia pull the lapels of her suit jacket tighter. "I don't know that I want to practice law anymore," she said softly.

Annabelle settled back on the bench and stared off toward the children riding the swings. "That's a big decision." Her voice was calm, reasonable, but Mia had seen the alarm flash in her eyes.

She thought Mia was being impulsive. Crazy, really. Who went through three grueling years of law school, was lucky enough to work at a firm like Pearson and

Stern, and then walked away from it all? Certainly not a sane person. Her parents were going to have the same reaction. God, she dreaded telling them. This was good practice.

"You're right. It's a huge decision. Not one I'm taking lightly."

"I should hope not." Annabelle frowned thoughtfully. "What would you do?"

"You've heard me mention my friends Lindsey Shaw and Shelby Cain. In college we'd talked about starting a concierge and rental business. Our sorority participated in a fundraiser where we all rented ourselves out for a day to run errands, cook, babysit, host a dinner—whatever the client needed for a specific occasion." She shrugged. "Not only did we have a blast, but we also could see the potential for some sort of full-service business in Manhattan."

"Sounds rather dangerous."

Mia smiled. "We'd make sure our clients are properly vetted. Besides, I figure the larger part of our business will be about renting designer purses and bridal gowns, that sort of thing. If kids from the local colleges want to sign up, we'd hire them for the concierge side. Our motto will be 'You can rent anything at Anything Goes.' Hey, maybe you'll want to rent out Mr. Muffin."

Annabelle smiled, but her expression remained troubled. "Your friends, they're willing to quit their jobs and move here?"

Mia sighed. That was going to be tricky. "I haven't discussed any of this with them yet."

"Oh…" Annabelle seemed relieved. "So you truly haven't made up your mind yet."

The reaction shouldn't have bothered her, but Mia

couldn't ignore the sense of betrayal she felt. For some reason, she'd thought Annabelle might understand. Here was a woman who'd shunned convention, turned her back on marriage and children in pursuit of her career when women simply didn't dream of forging their own path.

"No," she lied. "I haven't made up my mind."

"Good. This is a very big decision. You mustn't be hasty and do anything while I'm gone." Annabelle reached over and squeezed her hand. "Don't walk away because of David."

Mia jerked back and blinked. "David? Why would you— He has nothing to do with this. I don't understand why you'd bring him up."

Contradicting Annabelle's gentle smile, her eyes gleamed shrewdly. "Of course. Forgive a doddering old lady."

"David's my boss, nothing more."

The woman nodded.

"The only reason you ever heard about him was because we worked a few cases together." She paused, frustrated that she was feeling defensive. So, she talked about work sometimes. It was only natural that his name had come up. It wasn't as if the man noticed her. She was just one among the many, a useful tool, a worker bee. He hadn't even so much as shared a pizza with her when they'd been stuck late at the office. As if there could ever be something between her and David. The idea alone was laughable.

Annabelle lifted her face to the sun, her eyes closed, an annoying smile tugging at the corners of her mouth.

1

MIA WAITED UNTIL the waiter had poured the champagne into her friends' glasses before she raised her flute. "To us," she said, grinning at Lindsey and Shelby. "We did it."

"Yes, we did," Lindsey agreed, her mouth twisting wryly and her expression not looking quite as enthusiastic as Mia's or Shelby's. "We now owe more money than any three twenty-eight-year-old women should owe in their lifetimes."

Shelby laughed and downed her champagne.

"You're such a pessimist." Shaking her head, Mia elbowed her. "If we didn't think we could make a go of this, none of us would've signed on the dotted line, much less have quit our jobs."

"You did?" Lindsey's eyes widened. "Seriously? You've turned in your resignation already?"

"It's typed up and will be on my boss's desk tomorrow morning." Mia swallowed around the lump in her throat, the one that seemed to swell every time she thought about pulling out all of her savings and having no income until their new venture turned a profit. She glanced at Shelby. "What about you?"

"I was just waiting to sign the loan documents. I'll turn in mine on Monday as soon as I get back to Houston." Shelby snatched the pricey bottle of Cristal out of the ice bucket and refilled her glass. "We might as well enjoy this. After tonight, it's gonna be the cheap stuff for us until we make some dough."

Lindsey made a small whimpering sound, her blue eyes clouding. "Don't remind me."

Mia set down her flute, prepared to give the pep talk she'd been rehearsing for the past few weeks. Once she'd made up her mind that she wanted to leave her firm and take a chance on starting the new business, she'd leaned hard on Lindsey and Shelby, so to some degree she felt responsible for the other two taking the plunge with her. Plus she already lived in Manhattan. Her friends had to make the move, but they missed one another, and wanted to live in New York together.

"Oh, it won't be that bad," Shelby said, urging her to take another sip. "We'll eat and drink well when we go out on dates."

Mia cleared her throat. "About that…"

Both women looked expectantly at her.

"Unlike the glory days of college, Manhattan isn't exactly teeming with eligible men."

"Well, neither is Chicago." Lindsey sighed. "I haven't had a real date in seven months." She lifted her brows accusingly at Shelby, who never seemed to lack company of the male persuasion. "Maybe we should've moved to Houston, Mia. If things got too bad, at least we could count on leftovers."

Shelby waved dismissively. "Oh, sweetie, you're de-lusional if you think I've had any better luck there."

Lindsey snorted. "Right."

Mia eyed her friend. "Really, Shelby?"

"Really," she answered defensively, and then shrugged. "I can't remember the last time I went out a second or third time with the same guy and those are the dates that count." She sniffed. "And no, it's not because I'm too picky."

"You have every reason to be damn picky. We all do," Mia said and meant it, even though she was in the middle of a particularly long dry spell. It was mainly her fault. All those ungodly hours spent in the office hadn't helped. And if she were totally honest with herself, she'd spent too much time hoping David would finally man up, ask her out, share one lousy dinner with her. Despite what she'd told Annabelle, despite what she'd told her-self, she'd honestly thought he'd been attracted to her, at least in the beginning. Sadly, she'd clearly been fooling herself. No use thinking about him now.

"Amen." Lindsey downed a healthy sip. "Still would be nice to have an assortment to be picky over." She narrowed her eyes at Mia. "What ever happened to that guy you worked with? David, right?"

Mia nearly choked on her champagne. "There was never anything there."

"Yeah, I remember him," Shelby chimed in. "When you first started with the firm you thought he was hot."

"He is hot. Unfortunately, he's taken."

"Married?" Lindsey observed sympathetically.

"To the job. His father and uncle founded the firm, and the guy still puts in more hours than anyone else."

Mia shook her head. "Anyway, there's a rule about fraternization. God knows David Pearson would rather be strung up by his thumbs than step one toe over the line."

Lindsey giggled a bit, which told Mia the bubbly was getting to her friend, then grabbed the champagne and topped up everyone's glasses. "This is what I don't get…when we were in school there were all kinds of guys around. If we didn't have a date, it was because we didn't want to go out."

"I know, right?" Shelby frowned thoughtfully. "Even when we went out in groups, guys always outnumbered us. So what the hell happened to them? They can't *all* be married and living in the burbs."

"You have a point." Mia sipped slowly, worried that the alcohol was getting to her, too. Usually she wasn't such a lightweight, but she hadn't eaten anything all day. "Even during spring break, I swear, there were two guys to every girl."

"I'm the accountant," Lindsey said. "I'd say more like three to one."

"Junior year. Fort Lauderdale." Shelby slumped back in her chair, her expression one of total bliss. "Oh, my God."

"Are you kidding?" Mia stared at her in disbelief. "Come on. Senior year, Waikiki Beach, hands down winner."

Shelby's sigh said it all.

Lindsey smiled broadly. "Yep."

Along with the other two, Mia lapsed into silence, enjoying the heady memories of that magical week. She sipped her champagne as a notion popped into her head.

"Hey, guys," she said, her pulse picking up speed as the thoughts tumbled. "I have an idea."

"Oh, no." The ever cautious Lindsey glanced dramatically at Shelby. "I don't know if I can take another one."

"No, this is good." Mia grinned. "There's no law that says spring break is just for college kids."

"Okay." Shelby drew out the word.

Lindsey just frowned.

"We're going to be working our asses off until we get Anything Goes off the ground, right? If we want to take a vacation, this is the time. Probably the last time for years. Who knows, maybe we'll even get laid." Mia saw the interest mount in Shelby's face.

Not Lindsey. Her frown deepened. "Hawaii?"

"Why not?" Mia noticed the empty champagne bottle and signaled the waiter.

"Because it's too expensive, for one thing. Are you forgetting we've just signed our lives away?"

"I don't know." Mia sighed, not quite willing to give up the idea. "Maybe we can go on the cheap, pick up one of those last-minute deals. And none of us has officially put in our resignations. I'd be willing to work another two weeks at the firm if it meant enough money for Hawaii."

"It wouldn't hurt to see what's available," Shelby said.

"I suppose not." Lindsey set down her glass, not looking at all convinced. In fact, she stared at Mia as if she were a traitor. "But we'd have to set a budget first. A firm budget."

Mia nodded in agreement. The whole thing was ridiculous, and even if they did stay at their current jobs a bit longer, a Hawaiian vacation was pretty extravagant for three women who were about to give up their incomes and live on hope and dreams until they got their feet planted again. It shocked her that she'd even thought of it, let alone was actually considering such a crazy thing. She was normally far more sensible, for God's sake.

But damn it, she'd worked hard for the past six years, first in law school and then at Pearson and Stern. She deserved the break, and right now, with the cold March air whipping around outside, Hawaii sounded like a slice of heaven.

"You know what would be really cool?" Shelby's eyes lit up as she leaned forward. "Remember those three guys we met at that party on our last day on Waikiki beach?"

"Uh, yeah," Mia said. "Smokin' hot."

Lindsey stiffened. "What about them?"

"What if we could get them to meet us?" Grinning, Shelby darted a mischievous look between them. "In Hawaii."

"How would we do that? We don't even know their last names." Mia snorted. "Not to mention they're probably married or in prison."

Shelby gave Mia a look, then ignored her completely. "We know what university they went to, so we use Facebook."

"Huh." Mia thought for a moment. "We could send a message to the alumni group. It couldn't hurt."

"But they'll have to have signed up as alumni to get the message." Lindsey didn't seem thrilled.

Shelby shrugged. "Lots of people do. I have, haven't you?"

Mia shook her head. "Look, they answer, they don't, so what? It's Waikiki. We're bound to meet some gorgeous surfers who'll be ready to party," she said, warming to the idea.

"I like it." Shelby dug in her purse and produced a pen. "Anybody have a piece of paper or a dry napkin?"

Mia pulled her day planner out of her leather tote and tore off a used page. "Here."

"Oh, my God, they still have those things around. Why don't you use your BlackBerry?" Shelby found a clean spot on the table and started writing.

"I do both," Mia said, and glanced at Lindsey, who understood about being careful. She did not look happy.

"Okay, how about something like this…" Shelby squinted as if she were having trouble reading her own writing, which was awful. No one could ever read it but her. "Here we go—'Remember spring break? Mia, Lindsey and Shelby will be at the Seabreeze Hotel during the week of whatever. Come if you dare. You know who you are.'"

"Not bad, but we'll have to be more specific." Mia did a quick mental calculation. 'Remember Spring Break 2004.'"

"Right." Shelby scribbled in the correction. "Lindsey, what do you think?"

She shoved a hand through her blond hair and exhaled a shaky breath. It was dim in the bar, but Mia could see she was blushing. "I think you'll have to change Lindsey to Jill."

Shelby blinked. "You didn't give him your real name?"

With a guilty smile, Lindsey shook her head.

Mia and Shelby exchanged glances, and burst out laughing.

DAVID PEARSON PASSED Mia's empty office on his way to the conference room where he'd been summoned by his father and uncle.

He still couldn't believe she was gone. The day she'd handed him her letter of resignation had been a shock. Now, two weeks and three days later, he still couldn't come to grips with Mia no longer being with the firm. That she wouldn't be stepping off the elevator each morning, early, before anyone but himself had arrived at the office, her green eyes still sleepy, her shoulder-length dark hair still down and damp. By eight, she'd have drunk three cups of coffee—no cream, a little sugar—and pulled her now dry hair back into a tidy French twist. He'd known her routine and habits almost as well as he knew his own.

"Good morning, Mr. Pearson."

He looked blankly at the receptionist. Only then did he realize he'd stopped and had been staring at the plant Mia had left behind that was sitting near her office door. He silently cleared his throat. "Good morning, Laura."

Smiling, the pretty young blonde continued toward the break room with a mug in her hand.

"Laura."

"Yes?" she said, turning back to him.

"Will Mia be picking up this plant?"

She blinked. "I don't know. I don't think so."

"Well, something has to be done with it," he said more gruffly than he intended. He never got involved in such petty matters. Even more annoying was the unexpected hope that he'd see her again. "Either have it sent to her or if she doesn't want it, let someone take it."

"Mia's going to Hawaii. I'll keep it watered for now."

"Hawaii?" His chest tightened. "She's moving?"

"I bet she wishes." Laura grinned. "According to Lily, she'll be gone for a week."

"When is she leaving?"

The curiosity gleaming in the young woman's eyes brought him to his senses.

"Never mind." He shifted the file folders he'd been holding and started again toward the conference room. "Just do something with the plant."

"In a couple of days," Laura called after him. "She's leaving in a couple of days...I think."

David didn't respond, but kept walking. What the hell was wrong with him? It was none of his business what Mia did. She'd quit. Thanked him for the opportunity to have been part of the firm, told him she would be pursuing other endeavors, and that was it. He hadn't tried to talk her into staying. She was a damn good attorney, and he should have. But mostly he'd been too stunned.

The conference-room door was closed, and he knocked briefly before letting himself in. At one end of the long polished mahogany table sat his father, his uncle Harrison and Peter, one of the equity partners. Odd enough that his father would be in the office instead of on the golf course on a Friday, but all three men looked grim.

"Good morning, gentlemen."

"David." Peter nodded.

"Have a seat, David" was all his father said.

His uncle poured some water from a carafe on the table and pushed the glass toward David. "You'll want to add a shot of Scotch to that in a minute."

"What's going on?" As he slowly lowered himself

into one of the sleek leather chairs, he looked from one bleak face to the next.

"We've lost the Decker account," his father said, his complexion unnaturally pale.

David felt as if the wind had been knocked out of him. Thurston Decker was their second biggest client. "How?"

"That's not all," his uncle added, his features pinched. "It looks as if Cromwell may jump ship, as well."

Bewildered, David looked to Peter, who was staring at his clenched hands. "I don't understand." David shook his head. "They've both been with us for two generations without a single complaint. We've done an excellent job for them."

"They don't dispute that." His father removed his glasses and carefully began cleaning the lenses. "They're citing the economy."

"That's bull." Harrison angrily ran a hand through his graying hair. "It's Thurston's grandkids who're responsible. Those greedy little bastards. They're edging the old man out of the company and making a bunch of jackass changes."

"No point in getting steamed," David's father said wearily. He rarely got angry or displayed much emotion. David was much like him in that way. "We need to focus on bringing them back around."

"I doubt that's a possibility," Peter opined. He was a quiet, studious man, who'd joined Pearson and Stern a year before David, and arguably knew more about what was going on in the firm than either of the two senior partners. "I heard that Fritz Decker, the oldest grandson, has already hired one of his former prep school buddies who bought in to Flanders and Sheen. And for a much smaller retainer."

"How reliable is that information?" David asked.

Peter's mouth twisted wryly. "We can forget about Decker's business."

"Jesus Christ, what the hell happened to loyalty?" Harrison exhaled sharply and eyed David. "You might not know this, but your grandfather had just started this firm when Thurston Decker got into the booze business. He started out with one store and a bar. When he got tangled up with a moonshiner, your granddad took him on as a client for next to nothing."

David had heard the story and just nodded. "What about Cromwell? Did we screw up, or is he playing the economy card, too?"

Peter shrugged. "We didn't do anything wrong."

"Do we have a chance of wooing him back?"

"Good question." His father put on his glasses. "We've lost a few smaller clients in the past couple of months, legitimately as a result of the economy, and nothing that would ordinarily concern us, but at this juncture, throw Decker and Cromwell into the pot and we're in trouble."

David sank back in his chair, his head feeling as if it weighed a ton. He never thought he'd see this day. Pearson and Stern had been a reputable, prestigious firm his entire life. "What happens now?"

"We cut back," his father said. "No more weekly fresh flower deliveries, and the daily catering for the break room and conference rooms are to stop. You'd be as shocked as I was at how much those two items alone will save us."

"What about layoffs?" Peter asked.

The question startled David, especially when neither his father nor his uncle balked. He hadn't dared allow his imagination to go that far. Naturally he understood this was serious, but there had been other lows in Pearson and Stern's history and they'd always taken pride in keeping every one of their employees. "Layoffs? Surely we're not at that crossroad. We haven't tried to drum up more business yet."

"Not quite true. Your uncle and I have made some calls, but we've come up empty."

David stared at the defeated look on his father's tired face, and the heaviness in his chest grew. It wasn't just his reasoned approach to business that made David admire the hell out of his dad. He'd always been a fair employer, a dignified member of the bar association, and David was glad that he'd recently been able to pull back from the office to spend some much deserved time on the golf course. "I can make some calls, too," he said, withdrawing his BlackBerry from his pocket. "A couple of my old law professors from Harvard should be able—"

"David. Wait."

He glanced up.

"There is something you can do. That sharp young attorney, Mia."

"Mia Butterfield," Peter clarified.

"Right." Lloyd Pearson leaned forward. "There is a potential new client considering our firm. A very big client, who requires the administration of a rather large charitable foundation. That means a hefty retainer and billable hours for two to three full-time attorneys."

"What does this have to do with Mia?" David asked, confused. "You do know she no longer works here."

"Sadly, yes, because the new client has stipulated that Ms. Butterfield be in charge of the account."

"That makes no sense. Mia never did estate planning." David exhaled. "We have a stable of extremely talented tax and estate-planning attorneys. Or I could take on this new account myself."

His father shook his head. "I'm afraid not having Mia Butterfield handle the account is a deal-breaker, and no, there was no further explanation. You worked most closely with her. You'll have to convince her to come back."

"I doubt that's possible." He vividly remembered the day she'd delivered her letter of resignation. She'd stayed while he read it, then without hesitation on her part or even a trace of regret she was out the door.

"Offer her a bonus, a promotion, certainly a raise. Whatever it takes. We need this business, David, or we bring out the chopping block."

David loosened his tie and sank back. It was no use denying he wanted to see her again. For an instant he had wondered if her leaving would end up being the best thing that could've happened.

Damn it. Yeah, he wanted to see her again all right. But not like this.

2

THE HOTEL HADN'T CHANGED much in six years. Which was a very good thing because why mess with perfection? The lobby was airy and open, the fragrant scent of exotic flowers and salt water carried on the breeze that never failed to cool Mia off no matter how warm and humid the air.

She and Lindsey were headed to the Plantation Bar—by way of the sundry store to pick up a pair of sunglasses Lindsey had forgotten to pack—when they spotted Shelby walking through the lobby, alongside a bellman who carried her two designer bags.

"Look at her. She's already tanned," Lindsey said, shaking her head. The short pink sundress bared her shoulders and most of her legs, and a few more highlights had been added to her tawny-colored hair. She looked relaxed and happy, as if she'd already been here a week. So Shelby.

"Tanning salon," Mia murmured and lifted a hand to get their friend's attention. Mia had planned on using a tanning bed, too, but there had been no time. Up until her final day at Pearson and Stern she'd worked feverishly to make sure all loose ends were tied up and her one open case had been seamlessly turned over to one of the other junior associates. Then there had been some advance orders to place for the new business. Life had been hectic.

"Shoot, I worked up until the last minute," Lindsey said. "I didn't even have time to pick up some bronzing lotion."

"I'm just glad we got some sleep on the plane." They'd met up in Chicago and flown together directly to Honolulu. Since Shelby left from Houston, she'd come on her own. Having company, though, hadn't mattered much to Mia or Lindsey. After chatting for half an hour, they'd both crashed for most of the flight.

"Aloha." Shelby greeted them with a grin, her teeth particularly white against her tan face.

Mia noticed that she'd gotten a manicure, pedicure— the works—while Mia had been lucky to squeeze in a hair trim. "I hate you," she said, eying Shelby's strappy gold sandals and pretty pink toenails. "I really do."

"Thank you." Shelby glanced down at her tanned legs and feet. "I found the sandals yesterday. On sale, too."

"We've already checked in," Lindsey said, exchanging a glance with Mia. They both still wore their travel clothes, jeans and light sweaters, because Chicago had been nippy when they'd left that morning. "We scored adjoining rooms but they won't be ready for another hour or two."

"A whole hour? Bummer." Shelby made a face, and then smiled prettily at the bellman. "Kimo, do you think we'll really have to wait that long?"

His brown face split into a grin, and then he winked. "The assistant manager is my cousin. Let me see what

I can do." He put down the bags and set off on his mission.

His uniform included white shorts, and the three of them ogled his fine ass and muscled calves as he walked unhurriedly toward the front desk.

"I forgot how disgustingly healthy everyone looks around here, even in winter," Mia idly observed.

"And how everyone seems to be related," Lindsey said, and then turned to Shelby. "What a shameless flirt you are. Not that I'm not totally jealous."

A smug smile curved Shelby's lips. "Do you know if any of the guys showed up yet?"

Mia shrugged. "We were headed to the bar. If they're here, they might be hanging out there or at the pool."

"Oh, God." Alarm widened Shelby's hazel eyes. "You can't go on the prowl dressed like that."

"The prowl?" Mia laughed.

Lindsey rolled her eyes.

"Too bad we don't know their last names," Shelby said, "so we could see if they checked in." Her gaze drifted past her friends. "Although if they don't show, I see a couple of damn fine consolation prizes coming this way. No, don't turn—"

Lindsey whipped her head around, and then abruptly turned back to Mia, her cheeks red when the two buff dudes wearing only swim trunks smiled at them.

"Subtle, sweetie. Real subtle," Shelby whispered, her gaze averted, her lips barely moving.

"I'm going to get sunglasses," Lindsey muttered.

Mia elbowed her. "Wait, here comes Kimo."

The bellman approached, holding up three key cards.

"You're a doll, baby," Shelby told him, taking the

cards from him and flashing one of her trademark smiles, before passing two cards to Mia and Lindsey. "Um, Linds?" Shelby whispered, leaning close to her friend, "you might want to get some bronzing lotion along with those sunglasses."

FRESHLY SHOWERED and feeling rested from her nap on the plane, Mia left the other two to unpack and stake their territories while she went in search of an umbrella drink. The pool bar was packed with half-dressed people, lots of couples, but the Plantation Bar, which featured a view of the ocean, was shady, breezy and perfect. She slid onto a stool and studied the tented menu of exotic drinks.

The three of them sharing two adjoining rooms with a small parlor had sounded great in theory. It meant they had only two bathrooms, and while that setup had been fine in college, she was so not used to sharing anymore. But it was only for a week, and she wasn't planning on spending much time in the room. Especially if spring-break Jeff showed up.

And if he didn't…oh, well. She'd promised herself she wouldn't be bummed if their Facebook shout-out went unanswered. Even if Jeff did show up, he might not be as tall as she remembered, or broad and hunky with thick sun-kissed hair. She couldn't recall if he'd told her what his major had been, or if he'd shared his interests or much of anything else. They'd both been tipsy that night they met at the pool party—him more than her—and there had been a lot more kissing than conversation.

The swarthy, smiling bartender approached to take her order, and she settled on a blue fruity concoction, based solely on the pretty picture, and then swiveled around to gaze toward the beach. Aside from more couples stretched out on beach towels, there were a few groups of guys, but they looked young. One dude wearing a pair of red floral swim trunks and no shirt caught her attention. He was standing at an outside table where the bar met the sand. He had the same build as Jeff, except this guy's hair was a bit darker and shorter.

"Here you go," the bartender said, and she twisted around to find the tall, frothy drink garnished with a cherry, pineapple wedge and yellow paper umbrella. "Do you want to sign this to your room or keep a tab open?"

"I'll sign for it now." She grinned at the fancy cocktail. She wouldn't be caught dead ordering something this froufrou in Manhattan.

She plucked the cherry first and popped it into her mouth before using both hands to pick up the odd-shaped glass. The only other people sitting at the bar was a couple huddled at the far end who'd been talking to the bartender. As she struggled with her first sip, determined to leave the pineapple wedge undisturbed, she noticed a man pulling out a stool at the other end of the bar close to the wall. Tall, short dark hair, cream-colored shirt.

Frowning, she set the glass back down. Even though she hadn't actually gotten a good look at him, there was something oddly familiar about the way he moved, the way he…

Her heart somersaulted.

David.

Ridiculous, of course. It wasn't him. Couldn't possibly be. Not in this universe. Damn it. She had promised herself she wouldn't think of him once on this vacation, and she'd blown it in the first two hours.

For peace of mind she had to take another look. Trying to be inconspicuous, she used her cocktail napkin to wipe up an imaginary spill and slid a sidelong look at him.

It couldn't be. Except…it was.

Holy crap.

David smiled, and lifted his hand in a wave.

She blinked. Hard. He was still there. She'd never seen him in anything but a suit before. Certainly never seen him smile like that. David Pearson actually looked a little nervous. But that was impossible. In fact, this was nuts. What could he possibly be doing here?

"Mia?"

She blinked again, felt the heat of someone close behind her. A hand touched her shoulder, and she slowly turned.

"Mia, right?" It was red-swim-trunks guy.

She stared blankly at him, her mind still on David.

"It's Jeff."

"Jeff. Right. Of course." She looked into his familiar blue eyes and forced a smile.

He gave her a lopsided grin, ducked and zeroed in for a kiss on the mouth.

She turned her head just in time. The wet sloppy smooch landed on her cheek. His beer-saturated breath nearly knocked her over.

"Sorry," he mumbled, taking a second to right himself. "I wasn't sure you'd show up. I couldn't believe it when I read your post on Facebook. That was wild."

Mortified that David had seen what had happened, she leaned back, trying to put some distance between her and Jeff, who took the hint and sat on the stool beside her, fortunately not too close and blocking her view of David.

"When did you get here?" she asked, scrambling to concentrate.

"Yesterday morning. Me and two of my buddies. We got too much sun yesterday and spent more time than we should have at the bar today." He smiled sheepishly. "You just get in?"

"A couple of hours ago. My friends are still unpacking."

The bartender came for Jeff's order, and she was relieved when he asked for a soft drink. Though she was disappointed that mentioning her friends hadn't prompted him to volunteer whether his two buddies were the ones Lindsey and Shelby were expecting. She glanced at his friends and pretty much figured it out on her own. They didn't look the least bit familiar, and boy, were they not the right type.

Her gaze went back to Jeff and she found his bloodshot eyes fixed intently on her. "You look the same," he said, sounding relieved. "Your hair is shorter."

"Yours, too."

"Yeah." He self-consciously rubbed the back of his neck. "Good ol' corporate America."

"Jeff."

His friends hollered from across the bar, and when he turned to acknowledge them, she shot a look toward David. His seat was vacant, his glass half-empty. Her gaze shifted in time to catch a glimpse of his back as he left the bar.

"Look, we've rented surfboards," Jeff said, signaling for his check. "You wanna come?"

"Maybe another day."

"How about dinner?" Jeff lightly touched her hand and gave her the boyishly charming smile that had gotten to her six years ago. "You have plans yet?"

Her wistful gaze drifted helplessly toward the stool where David had been sitting only seconds ago. What was he doing here? It made no sense. Whatever the reason, it couldn't have anything to do with her. He probably hadn't given her a moment's thought since she'd left. As soon as it was announced that she'd given her notice, nearly everyone had tried to talk her into staying with the firm. But not David. He hadn't said a single damn word. This was simply a coincidence. A bizarre crazy coincidence. "No," she said finally. "No, I don't have plans."

"I'll make reservations someplace nice, and call your room when I get back. Okay?"

"Sure. I'm looking forward to it." She didn't even mind when he kissed her cheek.

DAVID HOPED HE WASN'T hanging around the lobby like an idiot for nothing. He checked his watch, then for the second time in five minutes, looked at his BlackBerry for messages, while mentally cursing his own stupidity. For God's sake, he knew why she was here. He'd overheard the ladies talking in the break room about Mia and her friends' plan to organize a reunion or some such thing relating to their senior year spring break.

Frankly it had sounded odd to him, not at all like something Mia would be involved in. He thought back to his own spring break, the last one before going to law school, and smiled. He and three friends had gone to Barbados for the week, where there had been a lot of women, too much drinking and not a shred of common sense among them. Twice they'd had to buy their way out of sticky situations with the local authorities.

Though nothing to be proud of, he wouldn't have traded that wonderful, reckless carefree week for anything. Everyone needed that rite of passage. A few months later, he'd been firmly embedded in law school, studying his ass off, and doing the Pearson name proud. He hadn't veered off course since, and he certainly wouldn't pull an adolescent stunt like trying to recreate the week.

Hard to believe Mia was part of this at all. She was a damn fine lawyer, a sensible, focused woman. He admired that about her, and so much more. She was poised and sexy and had the most incredible green eyes that had the damning effect of turning his insides to butter. Which made him twice the fool for having followed her here.

No one at the firm knew he was here, except his father and uncle, and neither had said a word about him taking off in search of Mia. In fact, they had breathed a sigh of relief that he was on the case. Only David had known that he wasn't in Hawaii to gain a client, no matter how desperately the company needed the influx of cash. He had come to see Mia for himself.

In the short time since she'd given her notice, too many of his thoughts had been regrets. He'd hidden his feelings for her for so long, he'd almost convinced himself that she didn't fill him with want. He'd cursed the fact that she worked for his firm, which made her off-limits. Now, when his opportunity was finally here, when there would be no negative repercussions if he asked her out, he couldn't. Not if he wanted to save a lot of jobs.

He didn't even know if it mattered. She might have no interest in him. He was boring, serious, a drill sergeant. He'd heard the nicknames too often when his employees had thought they were alone. David had no reason to think Mia would want to see him now.

But he needed to know. Once and for all. If she laughed in his face, it would be a good thing. He'd be able to stop thinking about her, fantasizing about that beautiful body. That quick wit. What might have been. Sure it would hurt, but not forever.

He needed to know before he asked her to come back to the firm. Before it became a moot point. Again.

He checked his watch. If she didn't show up within the next three minutes, it meant she was still hanging out at the bar with her new friend, and David would be wise to think about taking the next flight back to New York.

As soon as Jeff left, Mia drained her drink, and headed through the lobby toward the elevators. The first thing she was going to do was find out if David was registered at the hotel. If not, she'd call Suzie, an admin assistant who'd started with Pearson and Stern about the same time as Mia, and find out what the woman knew about why David was here. She was older and married with two children, and unlike most of the associates and admin staff at the firm, she had a life. Mia could trust Suzie to be discreet.

She didn't make it to the elevators.

"Mia." Suddenly David was right in front of her, a couple of feet away. If she'd turned left instead of right…

"David." Her breath caught at the wedge of exposed chest hair where his tennis shirt came to a *V*. She'd never seen him without a tie. Not once. He was always impeccably dressed in his tailored suits, with his black hair perfect, his eyes so serious. "What are you doing here?"

"Vacation."

"You never take vacations."

"Not true."

"Four-day weekends occasionally."

He shrugged. "I needed some time off."

"You're right. This is good." She cleared her throat as she looked away. Of course she *felt* discombobulated. That didn't mean she had to show it. "Are you here with someone?"

"No, alone." He smiled, faint lines fanning out at the corners of his brown eyes. "Not counting you."

She tried to hide her unsteady hands in her pockets, fumbling with the folds of material until she remembered she had no pockets, not in the short halter dress she wore. So instead of disguising her nervousness, she'd drawn his attention to her legs. Her very pale legs.

"How about you?" he asked, lifting his gaze to hers. "Are you here with that guy in the bar?"

"Him? No." She laughed dismissively. "With Lindsey and Shelby. I don't think you know them."

His mouth curved into another smile, and it stunned her how much it changed his face. The man had incredible dimples. His eyebrows lifted along with his grin, and he looked ten years younger.

"No, I don't think you ever mentioned them," he said.

She didn't roll her eyes, although she wanted to. Of

course he didn't know them. Had they ever once discussed anything personal? Not for one hot second.

"Have you ever been here before?" he asked.

"A long time ago. For spring break."

"Ah." His slight frown confused her. "So you'd know some of the good restaurants? Hot spots?"

Mia pressed her lips together, wondering what strait-laced David Pearson considered a hot spot.

He was still smiling, and she was still trying to get used to it. "Assuming you were in any condition to remember."

At that, she laughed. "Me?"

"Come on. Anyone who took off on spring break wasn't there to crack the books."

"Not even you?"

"Let's say I have a few stories I won't be telling my grandchildren."

"Well, well, Mr. Pearson, I see you in a whole new light."

He paused. "Good." The slow sensual curve of his lips made her heart trip. And his eyes, good God, the way he looked at her, as if she were the only person in the lobby. She couldn't speak. Could barely think. He was here alone…could that mean…this wasn't real… she was making stuff up…

"Hey! I thought I'd find you in the bar."

Coming from behind, Mia barely registered Shelby's voice.

"Mia? Oh, I'm interrupting. Sorry."

Mia blinked, glanced blearily at her friend. "Shelby. Hi."

Shelby smiled. "Hi." She swung a look at David, her

eyes full of amused curiosity as she sized him up. "I'm Shelby."

"David." He politely offered his hand as if he were meeting a new client for the first time.

The moment was gone. What was left was the same David she had known for three years.

"You're not interrupting. I was on my way up to the room," Mia said with a small shrug.

"Yeah, um…" Her gaze skittered briefly toward David then back to Mia. "Someone left you a message."

"Who?"

"It's about dinner."

"Already?" The word slipped out as she was unable to contain her surprise. Refusing to look at David, Mia's eyes met Shelby's. "This couldn't have waited?"

"Lindsey's out shopping and just texted." Shelby's mouth lifted in a sly smile. "She may be having company."

"Oh." Mia frowned, paused. "Oh," she repeated with enthusiasm. Lindsey had been certain her guy wouldn't show up. "Good." She sent an apologetic glance at David, and then a more probing one at Shelby, who gave a small sad shake of her head.

"Look, I'm the one who's interrupting," David said, taking a step back. "Maybe I'll see you around."

"No, wait." Great. Now what? They both faced Mia, waiting expectantly. "Let's all have dinner," she said, shocked at what had just come out of her mouth. Yet she'd feel awful deserting Shelby on their first night here. "David, Shelby, join Jeff and me. I'm sure he won't mind."

3

"ARE YOU SURE ABOUT THIS?" Shelby asked when she and Mia approached the designated restaurant two minutes early and saw that David was waiting outside. "He's absolutely gorgeous."

"If you ask me one more time, I swear I'll…" Mia finished with an exasperated grunt. The closer they got, the yummier he looked in crisp khakis and a white button-down shirt open at the neck. She hoped tonight wasn't a mistake, but she couldn't stand to think of Shelby being left alone, especially knowing that her guy wasn't coming, and that he was married with his first child on the way.

Shelby hadn't seemed particularly disappointed; of course, the girl always landed on her feet. She'd undoubtedly have men lining up in no time. Besides, David wasn't her type. But Mia had opened her big mouth, so too late. End of story.

"Still, I know you used to have a thing for him."

"Used to. Now shut up," Mia murmured as they got within hearing distance.

They both pasted on smiles, and the moment he

spotted them his smile came so easily that Mia had trouble believing this was the same guy she'd worked with for three years.

She'd always considered him attractive, with his dark hair and intense brown eyes. The first day they'd met he'd sent her pulse skittering, but his rare smiles and overall serious nature had bothered her. She'd understood to some degree why he'd kept up the barrier. He was a supersmart guy and one hell of a lawyer, but his high-ranking position with the firm at only thirty could have easily been interpreted as nepotism. He was thirty-three now. Time to relax. He'd proven himself many times over.

"You ladies look lovely," he said, giving them equal attention as he took in their new sundresses. "Would you like to be seated at our table, or wait out here for Jeff?"

"Let's sit down," Mia said, never having had trouble being decisive. "We should be able to see him when he gets here."

"Good." David gave the host a slight nod, and the man gathered menus and indicated they should follow him.

Shelby went first, and then David lightly touched the small of Mia's back for her to proceed. A triangular cutout at her waist exposed bare skin, allowing his fingertips to graze the sensitive area. Her entire body reacted. The tingling started at her nape and slithered down her spine. Goose bumps surfaced on her arms and back.

She picked up the pace so that contact was quickly broken, but he'd have to be blind not to see what his touch had done. The restaurant was outdoors, and even though it was twilight, strings of white lights were woven through the surrounding palm trees to illuminate the walkway—and reactions Mia preferred weren't so obvious.

They arrived at the table, an excellent one, private yet affording a breathtaking view of the water. She'd bet an expensive bottle of wine that David had greased the host's palm to get this baby.

The host pulled out a chair, and so did David. Shelby and Mia exchanged secret smiles as they settled in. David's manners didn't surprise Mia. Not once had she seen him sit or enter an elevator before a woman. He probably opened car doors, too, but she'd never had the opportunity to see him in action.

"Your server will be Cole. He'll be here shortly to offer you cocktails." The host passed out the menus, leaving the wine list with David. "In the meantime, is there anything else I can do for you?" he asked as he shook out Shelby's white linen napkin and draped it across her lap.

Shelby smiled and shook her head. Mia didn't bother. She knew the question was mainly addressed to David, who said, "I think we're fine for now. Thank you, Ryan."

"Oh." Mia stopped the man. "If you could be on the lookout for the fourth person who's joining us—"

"Of course." The glance at David told her he'd already taken care of that, too.

The situation was kind of weird for her. When she and her friends were out, she was usually the one in charge, or at least they automatically deferred to her.

"I could get used to this," Shelby said, surveying the other diners, mostly dressed in subdued aloha shirts and lightweight floral dresses. "Houston can be casual, especially in the summer when it's so hot, but this rocks."

David followed her gaze. "I'm practically overdressed."

Shelby grinned. "Feel free to take your shirt off."

Mia chuckled when David blinked, his normally expressionless face slightly startled. Nothing that came out of Shelby's mouth surprised her, but she doubted David was used to being teased. That's why she didn't feel threatened by Shelby, who looked too damn cute in her strapless yellow dress. She simply wasn't his type.

There. She'd acknowledged the evil little thought that had consoled her after she'd foolishly suggested David and Shelby come to dinner.

"Think I could get away with it?" David asked, his eyes filling with warm amusement.

Shelby laughed. "What's the worst that can happen?" She shrugged her bare bronzed shoulders. "They'll ask you to put it back on."

"I think I'll let a braver soul than me test the boundaries of their dress code." His gaze met Mia's.

She forced a smile. How could she have underestimated Shelby? It wasn't that she blamed her for being so charming and irresistible.

"So, Shelby—" David set the wine list aside "—I understand you went to school with Mia. Are you also an attorney?"

"No," she said with a startled laugh, as if that was a joke. "No offense. Nothing wrong with being a lawyer. I'm in PR. As soon as we get the business off the ground I'll be handling the publicity, advertising, networking, that sort of thing."

His brows went up, and Mia cringed inside. She

hadn't told him about Anything Goes. It wasn't as if it were a big secret. But David would never understand how she could walk away from the law to start a business like that.

He didn't ask the expected question, but rather stared past Mia. "I believe your date is here."

She swung a gaze toward the entrance, and there was Jeff headed toward them. He'd cleaned up nicely, having changed into white jeans and a blue Hawaiian shirt. He waved, acknowledging them, and then stopped to talk to a waitress carrying a full tray of food. With her chin, she gestured to a passing waiter, and after Jeff had a word with the guy, he finally joined them at the table.

"I'm not late, am I?" he asked, kissing Mia on the cheek before taking his seat beside her.

She immediately smelled the booze on his breath. Great. "We've only been here a few minutes."

Frowning and totally ignoring David, who'd gotten to his feet, Jeff's gaze skimmed the table. "They haven't served drinks yet."

"Our server is coming," Mia said tightly. "I don't know if you remember Shelby, and this is David."

"Jeff." David extended his hand. "Thanks for allowing us to join you."

Jeff half rose and accepted the handshake. "No problem. I should've brought my friends, too."

Mia tried not to shudder. She tried even harder not to look at David, who'd reclaimed his seat. Though maybe she was the only one who knew Jeff was slightly off.

"How did the surfing go?" she asked.

"Shit. I nearly broke my neck. Check this out." He yanked up the hem of his shirt to show where the skin across his ribs was beginning to bruise. "I banged up my back, too."

Oh, God. They didn't need to see that. "Bummer," Mia said, and picked up the leather-bound menu. "We should look at the menus."

Jeff dropped his shirt in place and craned his neck. "Where's our waiter? I gave him my drink order."

Mia glanced at Shelby and David. They both had taken her suggestion and were studying their menus. Neither of them seemed put off by Jeff, but they were probably just being polite.

The waiter arrived with Jeff's Scotch and an apologetic look for the rest of them, then he took everyone else's drink order. While they waited, Mia quickly decided on an entrée and urged Shelby with a pointed look to do the same. David diplomatically handled the selection of the wine, something Mia gladly would have skipped altogether.

Other than Jeff reaching under the table to squeeze her thigh, an attempt that was immediately rejected, the rest of the meal went smoothly enough. David and Shelby got along fabulously, chatting away as if they'd known each other for ages. Mia should've been grateful they were distracted, but their rapport only helped to darken her mood. She was jealous, and she had no one to blame but herself. And Jeff. Rational or not, she totally blamed him. Why did he have to turn out to be such an ass?

When the bill came, there was a brief struggle between David and Jeff. No surprise to her, David won. Any other time, Mia might have offered to pick it up herself since she'd invited Shelby and David, but all she wanted was to get back to her room. No way was she spending another minute with Jeff, who'd had a glass in his hand throughout dinner. Only one thing could make the night worse—if Shelby stayed out with David.

"Well," Mia said, after giving Jeff a firm send-off, and he'd started weaving his way toward the lobby. Or more likely, the next bar. "I'm beat."

Neither Shelby or David responded, and a lump swelled in Mia's throat. They'd gotten along much better than she'd anticipated. Who knew David could be that social and charming, damn him. She wouldn't be surprised if they wanted to spend more time together.

She swallowed hard. "Guess I'll catch up with you two tomorrow." Mia's gaze involuntarily flicked to David. He'd been watching her intently. She blinked at the sudden awkwardness. "Thanks for dinner. I should've foot the bill. I owe you one."

His warm chocolate-brown eyes stayed level with hers. "I'll remind you," he said, his voice a seductive murmur in the semidarkness.

Shivering with awareness, she rubbed her bare arm. She couldn't seem to look away. With a jolt of regret, she remembered Shelby was standing there watching.

Mia stepped back, avoiding a glance at her friend. And David. "Okay. I'm off to bed. See ya," she said breezily, knowing she wasn't going to sleep one lousy wink.

"Wait for me," Shelby said, and Mia stopped and cautiously turned. "I'm pretty jet-lagged myself. David, it was so nice meeting you. You're staying here, too, yes?" He nodded, and she added, "Then we'll see you around."

David's gaze briefly shifted in the direction that Jeff

had disappeared. "I wouldn't mind walking you to your rooms."

"We're fine, really." Shelby looped an arm through Mia's. Not a Shelby-like thing to do. "We're staying in rooms seven-twenty and seven-twenty-two. Give us a call tomorrow."

He nodded. "I just might do that. Good night, ladies."

Shelby gave Mia's arm a small tug, and they headed toward the elevators. "Do not turn around," Shelby whispered sternly. "I promise you he's watching."

"What?" Mia jerked her arm away. "Why would I turn around?" Any remorse she'd felt for stepping on her friend's toes disappeared in a flash. "You could've stayed out with him. I don't need an escort to my room, for God's sake."

Shelby only grinned.

"I should warn you. He's not always that charming. Frankly, I didn't know he had any personality. He's usually stuck in Neutral."

"Uh-huh." They'd arrived at the elevators and, still smiling, Shelby pressed the Up button.

"I'm not trying to discourage you. I'm not," Mia muttered. "I say go for it. I can see why you might be attracted. I was once."

Shelby laughed. "For being a brainy chick, you're such a dope."

Mia scowled at her, but kept her mouth shut when the elevator doors opened, and two couples exited.

"Get in there." Shelby pulled her into the car, and then waited for the doors to close. "Sweetie, he is so into you, it's pathetic."

"You're crazy. He was all Mr. Charming with you."

"He is charming. But you didn't see the way he was looking at you."

"No, he wasn't."

Shelby rolled her eyes. "You were too busy being embarrassed by Jeff. David wasn't obvious, he's too gentlemanly. But he didn't miss a single eyelash flutter. Trust me." She sighed. "Seriously, if he'd been eyeing me like I was a juicy steak, I'd be all over him."

Mia thought about it for a minute. "Then why wait and come all the way to Hawaii?"

"Yeah, Mia," Shelby said with a hand on her hip. "Why would someone, who never takes vacations, suddenly come all the way to Hawaii for a week? Tell me."

Excitement fluttered in her chest. "It is odd," she admitted. "All he had to do was pick up the phone while I was still in New York."

"Hey, hopping a plane at the last minute is a pretty grand gesture, don't knock it." The doors opened, and Shelby walked out first, her key already in hand. "And for God's sake, don't blow it."

DAVID PACED THE PARLOR of his suite. His body recognized East Coast time, where it was three in the morning and not 10:00 p.m. Hawaiian time. Add to that the twelve hours he'd spent in the air, he should've been exhausted. But he was too keyed up to sleep.

Even dinner had been draining. Shelby had been great company—witty, refreshingly open and quite beautiful. But it was Mia's attention he'd wanted, when her green eyes had locked with his. Instead he'd watched her helplessly act as buffer for that idiot Jeff. He'd pitied them both. Jeff, because he was too drunk to realize what he'd screwed up, and Mia, well, her evening had virtually been ruined.

David smiled ruefully. The upside for him was that he'd come out the victor. Or so he hoped. He still didn't know where he stood, whether he was a fool for showing up. Damn it, he should've stopped her from going to her room, asked her to have a drink alone with him.

He wasn't worried about hurting Shelby's feelings—it wasn't as if they'd been on a date. She was clearly a bright woman and knew what was what.

He slid open the glass door, walked to the balcony railing and stared at the city lights. Getting this last minute suite had been lucky. The corner unit provided both a view of the ocean and the Waikiki skyline. It also came with a well-stocked bar, or he could've ordered drinks from room service. Either way, Mia should've been enjoying this view with him right now.

Rooms 720 and 722. Weren't there three of them? Which room was Mia's? He could call the front desk, but they wouldn't give him her room number, only connect him. He had no desire to talk to her on the phone, he decided as he closed the balcony door behind him. He'd done enough talking. Enough dodging and evading for the past three years. Enough denying himself.

He grabbed his key card off the bamboo console table, and let himself out.

Enough was damn well enough.

TIRED OF PACING, Mia lay back on the queen-size bed closest to the bathroom, locked her hands behind her head and stared up at the ceiling. Occasionally she could hear Shelby rattling around in the next room. Mia knew she wanted to stay up chatting, and Mia felt only slightly guilty for not indulging her. The need for privacy won out.

Lindsey hadn't been in the room when they'd returned, and they suspected she might not show up again until morning. Good for her. Mia was dying to meet the guy Lindsey had been so tight-lipped about, but this was the first moment's peace she'd gotten since arriving, and she had a lot to think about.

David.

Good Lord, it still didn't seem real. Him. Here. Thousands of miles away from New York. To some degree it pissed her off that for three years he'd given her not one itty-bitty hint that he was attracted to her. Talk about cool, dispassionate, stoic. Great qualities if you're in the courtroom, but damn it, they'd spent far too many nights working late for him not to have cracked just a little.

So there was a "no fraternization" policy at the firm? So what that he was the heir apparent? He could've been human, showed a trace of emotion toward her. Then she could have decided what was more important, staying with the firm or seeing him. Who knew what could have developed by now?

What a coward. She had a good mind to go knock on his door and make him spell out why he'd come to Hawaii. Had he come for her or not? If not, fine. There was plenty of trouble she could get into all by herself. But if he had come for her…

She had to know, she decided, swinging her feet to the floor, even if it meant they had only this one week. In fact, if they reverted to their former relationship once they returned to New York, that would be perfect. All her focus and energy would be invested in the new company. She'd have no time for a relationship. All the more reason not to waste a minute now.

Her key wasn't where she'd thought she left it. Impatient, she dumped the contents of her purse onto the bed, then found the key card tucked safely in the side pocket, where she now recalled putting it. She checked her reflection in the mirror, applied some lip gloss, drew a brush through her hair and adjusted the bodice of her coral-colored dress. When she twisted around to inspect the back, her gaze snagged on the skin exposed by the triangular cutout. Where David's warm palm had been, had lingered until she'd pulled away.

Reliving the few seconds in her mind, she shivered. His hand hadn't been as soft as she expected. She knew he was an avid tennis player in his spare time, and that his mother was fond of arranging dates to accompany him to company dinners. Mia knew nothing more about his personal life. Among the paralegals and clerical help, there was some gossip and the occasional rumor, but she made a point to stay clear of the whispers.

Smoothing down her dress, satisfied that it wasn't too wrinkled, she palmed the key card and opened the door. And stopped cold.

David stood in the hall, staring at her. He seemed as surprised to see her as she was to see him. He wore the same clothes he'd worn at dinner, only his sleeves were rolled back, exposing his muscled forearms. Definitely a tennis player.

"I was about to knock," he said. "If you're on your way out—"

No way she'd let him weasel out of this. She opened her mouth to tell him just that, but he hadn't finished.

"I'll keep it brief." Without hesitation, he took a step

toward her, his lips twitching into what could only be described as a predatory smile.

"Okay," she said, trying to keep her voice from shaking.

Then he crossed the threshold and closed the door behind him, sending her scurrying backward with the inelegant grace of a beached whale.

4

"I HOPE YOU WEREN'T on your way to meet Jeff," David said. "If you are, it's a complete mistake."

Mia backed up another step, stopped, gave him a good long look, then laughed. "You came here to tell me that?"

"I did."

"For an overpaid attorney, you're not every observant."

He lifted his brows.

She hid a smile. "I meant high-priced."

"I know you were embarrassed at dinner, but that doesn't mean you wouldn't give him another chance." Again he advanced on her, and her pulse skittered. "The guy's a drunken lout. He's not good enough for you. Even if only for a week."

Heat crawled up her neck. He was right, of course, and she had no intention of doing more than exchanging a greeting with Jeff should she see him in the lobby. But David had no business butting in. "Since when are you an expert on my personal life?"

"Touché." He took her hand, slowly rubbed her palm with his thumb.

She tensed, but in a good way. Jesus, this was David touching her, his face so close that she could see the light flecks of amber in his brown eyes. Funny, she'd always thought they were much darker, more serious.

She straightened, tried to ignore the disturbing sensations his thumb caused. "In fact, Mr. Pearson, you really don't know anything about me, do you?"

His gaze touched her mouth, lingered and then leisurely moved up. "Don't I?"

"In the three years since we met, you haven't said anything more personal than 'Have a nice weekend.' And that was on a Saturday afternoon, after we'd worked most of the day together."

"You exaggerate."

"Not by much."

"You think it was easy, keeping my distance?"

"I honestly have no idea." Her breath caught at the flicker of amusement in his eyes. "You should've been a poker player, instead of a lawyer. You could've made a killing."

He wrapped his fingers around her hand and tugged her closer. "My intentions must be fairly obvious now," he said in a low, gravelly voice.

She tilted her head back, refusing to be the first to break eye contact as he slid an arm around her waist and pulled her against him. He was hard behind the fly of his khakis, the knowledge shattering a bit of her control. His hand splayed across the exposed skin of her lower back, and his palm felt hotter than it had before.

The tingling began there, traveled all the way up her spine and settled in her braless breasts, tightening her nipples, making them so sensitive that she could hardly stand to have them touch the light sateen material of her dress. Only a knot of fabric at her nape kept the halter in place. The gentlest pressure, the smallest tug...

He put his mouth on hers, his lips soft and supple, his breath minty. She moved against him, laid a hand on his chest, finding a surprising wall of muscle beneath the cotton fabric. When he drew his tongue across the seam of her lips, she parted them, inviting him inside.

David knew how to kiss—he was even better than she'd imagined. He smoothly dove in, but took his time, tasting, nibbling, touching his tongue to hers, giving her just so much, and then holding back until she trembled from wanting more. She pressed herself against him, pushed up to increase the pressure of his mouth. Her aroused nipples rubbed against his chest, and she thought for one dazed, hopeful second that he was about to untie her top.

But he only stroked her back, made a final sweep of the inside of her cheek. When he retreated, lingering long enough to touch his lips to hers one last time, she nearly whimpered in protest.

"I've wanted to do that for three years," he said, his voice husky, his eyes smoldering with a hunger that stole her breath.

"I didn't know," she whispered, her whole body weak. "You never showed it."

"No." With his thumb, he stroked her cheek. "I couldn't."

A part of her resented his ability to exercise that much control. She herself had struggled to keep her feelings in check, and too often she'd failed. How many times had she worried that other people in the office had noticed the lingering looks, the longing in her face? Especially that first year when she'd been too naive to understand that David would never breach company policy. Or finally to accept that he simply wasn't interested in her.

He lowered his head again, and brushed his lips across hers. Gently, almost too gently. Surely he didn't need a push. She was about to make it clear they wanted the same thing, even if she had to strip off his clothes, when he broke contact, moved back, out of reach.

"I've rented a car," he said, "and I plan on driving around the island tomorrow. I'd like for you to join me."

Her arms hanging loosely at her sides, her chest still heaving, she could only stare mutely at him. He'd reverted to the old David. Just like that. His face was unreadable, his eyes filled with that dark intensity that both excited and frustrated her. But the thing he couldn't hide was the bulge behind his fly.

"Naturally I understand if you already have plans." He stuffed his hands into his pockets and backed toward the door.

"No, um, not yet." She really hadn't had much to drink, maybe it was jet lag, but her head was fuzzy. She didn't get what was happening. "I'd love to go."

"Would nine-thirty be all right?"

"Nine-thirty. Sure."

"Let's meet in the lobby."

"Okay."

"I'm looking forward to spending time with you, Mia," he said. "Tomorrow, then."

"David—"

"Good night." He barely smiled, then left the room.

Mia stared at the closed door, wondering what the hell had just happened. Her lips weren't the only place still damp from his kiss. And he'd been as aroused as she. Ten more minutes and they would've been locking the adjoining door and diving between the sheets. She wanted it, and she knew he did, too.

Was he giving her time and space to consider what she was getting into? That would be totally like him. Sighing, she kicked off her sandals, and glanced at the digital bedside clock. Damn, she hoped she could get to sleep and not spend two hours replaying the last ten minutes.

She undid the bow at her nape, pausing to massage the tense muscles underneath when she heard her Black-Berry signal that she'd received a text. In her haste to grab the phone, she jammed her bare foot into the corner of the dresser and nearly broke her little toe. All for nothing. Disappointed, she read the text. It was from Lindsey—she didn't know if she'd be coming back to the room tonight. Good for her.

Mia muttered a mild oath and limped to the bed. What a waste. She had the room to herself, and David, the coward, had slunk away. That was the last time she'd let him off the hook. He'd already shown his hand by flying all the way to Hawaii. Tomorrow he'd better plan on doing more than sightsee.

DAVID ARRIVED IN the lobby fifteen minutes early and made arrangements for the car to be brought around before Mia showed up. He'd blown it last night, and didn't want to waste another minute of the six days he had left here.

No, he hadn't really squandered last night. He could easily have gotten her into bed. They both wanted it. They both knew it. Especially after that kiss. Which he also didn't regret, but couldn't think about now or risk embarrassing himself in front of a lobby full of Japanese tourists. He watched them, dressed in their aloha shirts and muumuus, cameras hanging from around their necks, chatting with their guide near the koi pond filled with orange and gold carp.

He envied their carefree excitement, their sole purpose as vacationers to enjoy the sparkling blue ocean, the balmy March air that came off the water. Ordinarily he never would have considered traveling this far for a vacation, or for that matter, staying away from the office for longer than three or four days unless it was work-related. But then, this wasn't actually a vacation.

It could have been, and God knew he wanted this time alone with Mia where they could forget about work and family obligations and get to know each other on a personal level. But hooking up with her wasn't that simple. Not now, not since his father had asked him to convince her to return to the firm.

He had to make her understand that he wanted to be with her, that he wasn't here just to lure her back. He could have talked to her in New York, offered her a nice bonus and promotion that she would've had to think twice about turning down. But he needed this break because by the time they returned, he wanted her to be clear on what she wanted, him or the firm.

Only problem was, it was a fine line. Once he extended the firm's offer, she'd have to trust that his motives were pure.

"David?"

He snapped out of his preoccupation. She stood right in front of him, and he hadn't even seen her walk up. "Mia."

"Bet you were thinking about work."

"Oddly, no."

She grinned. "Right."

He frowned at his watch. "I haven't even called the office, and it's what, one-thirty there."

"Go ahead. I'll wait."

"Nope. If they have a problem they can call me," he said, ignoring her skeptical expression and appreciating her brief white shorts and the long expanse of legs even more. "The car is parked right over here." He gestured at the red convertible, uncomfortably aware of how much he wanted to kiss her.

"Sweet." She took her sunglasses out of her bag and slipped them on as they walked toward the BMW. "Do you know where we're going?"

"I have a list of places."

"That's not an answer."

Unable to help himself, he touched the small of her back with a guiding hand, even though it was completely unnecessary. "I'll let you know when we get there."

She flashed him a smile, her teeth white, her lips a pale glossy pink. "I don't know how to navigate, so if you're counting on me..."

"The car has a GPS system."

"Ah." She lifted the hair off the back of her neck. "It's warmer than I thought."

Tempted to plant a kiss at her nape, he had to look away. "Only in the direct sun. We can put the top up if you want."

"No, I want to feel the wind in my face and in my

hair. It's Hawaii. I'm on vacation. I want it all," she said, giving him a look that made his cock twitch. "It might be a rumor, but I heard that what happens in Waikiki, stays in Waikiki."

"Right," he muttered, uncomfortably aware that he suddenly felt awkward. He never had trouble with women. No, it wasn't even that. He had a plan. Sex wasn't supposed to come first, but if she kept up the sly smiles and sultry looks, it was going to be murder keeping his head.

The valet who'd brought the car around trotted up and opened Mia's door before David could. "Need directions, sir?"

David shouldn't have been annoyed. The man was only doing his job, but David had missed out on watching her swing her long bare legs into the car. "No thanks," he said, slipping the man a ten before climbing in behind the wheel.

"I could get used to this." Mia adjusted her leather seat so that she partially reclined, and then tugged at the hem of her shorts.

He turned away and fiddled with the navigation system. "It drives well. I picked it up at the airport instead of taking a cab."

"I'll take your word for it. I have my license, but I've only driven twice since college."

He wasn't completely surprised. In Manhattan, he mostly took cabs himself. "What about weekends? Don't you like getting out of the city?"

Her eyebrows arched over her sunglasses, a cynical smile curving her lips. "Weekends? Is there such a thing at Pearson and Stern?"

"Point taken." He took out his sunglasses and slid them on before pulling out of the lot. "Is that why you left?"

"I never minded the work."

He cursed himself for bringing it up. Not so much because she sounded defensive, but the subject only reminded him of his unwanted errand. Luckily traffic was heavy and required all of his attention. So did the GPS. He already knew from studying the map earlier that Hawaiian street names were difficult to differentiate. Too many vowels.

She apparently got the message that he was focusing on driving, but as soon as they stopped at a red light, she asked, "The day I resigned...why didn't you ask why I was leaving?"

"I was too shocked."

"You had two and a half weeks."

David sighed. "I don't know why. Denial, maybe."

She didn't respond, but tied her hair back into a ponytail with something she'd found in her purse. "The light's green."

"Thanks." He started to proceed, but two pedestrians darted into the crosswalk, and he jammed on the brakes.

Mia gasped softly, her hand shooting out to brace herself. "And they say New York is bad."

"No kidding." He waited until it was clear, and then accelerated. "I keep forgetting you've been here before. I should've asked if there's someplace in particular you wanted to go."

"Uh, I didn't get too far out of Waikiki. Or off the beach, for that matter. I had the worst sunburn."

"I did the same thing freshman year, and I knew

better. When I was a kid we spent a lot of summers in Aruba and St. Thomas."

"Yeah, I know what you mean. That Caribbean sun is killer."

"Where did you summer?" he asked conversationally, then heard an odd strangling noise coming from her. He glanced away from the road long enough to see her burst out laughing.

"The backyard in a small blue inflatable swimming pool." She patted his arm. "That's where we Butterfields summered. On special occasions we went to our neighbor's backyard."

"All right." He felt like an idiot. "Consider me duly chastised."

"You get a pass, but only because you're not spoiled or a snob." She paused. "Contrary to what I thought when I first started with the firm."

He took his gaze off the road long enough to shoot her a look of disbelief. "Totally unfounded."

"Not from where I sat."

"On what grounds?"

"Oh, my God, you sound like a damn lawyer."

He smiled. "Guilty as charged."

"Okay, no more of that kind of talk."

"Or what? You'll fine me for contempt?"

Mia groaned. "The upside is that you do have a sense of humor, corny as it is. It wouldn't be enough that you're pretty."

He choked out a laugh. "Pretty?"

"Oh, come on." She drew a finger along his jaw. "You know you are."

All he knew is that if she didn't keep her hands to

herself, he'd end up rear-ending the Jeep in front of them. "Where did you grow up?"

She withdrew, though chuckled softly as if she knew he was trying to distract her. "Upstate New York. Ithaca, not too far from Cornell."

"But you didn't go there as I recall."

"Too expensive. I went to NYU." She'd moved her hand, or at least she wasn't touching him. "I'm surprised you know anything about my undergrad studies."

"I read your résumé."

"You weren't there for the interview process."

"I was in Atlanta overseeing a case." Good thing. He clearly remembered meeting her on her first day at the firm. One look into those sexy green eyes and he knew he wouldn't have hired her. "But I was the one who initially flagged you as a candidate."

"Hmm, I didn't know." She shifted, angling her knees toward him. "Why me? You probably had a dozen Harvard and Yale graduates nipping at your heels."

"We did."

"So what was it about my résumé that caught your attention?"

He cocked a brow at her. "You were only second in your class, but the top dog had already hired on with another firm in San Francisco."

"Thanks," she said dryly. "I happen to know you're full of it because Lance Heatherton went to work for his father." She sniffed. "And just so you know, he barely inched past me."

David smiled at her competitive streak. "Frankly, being second in your class obviously got our attention, but what impressed me more was that you were there on a scholarship, working a part-time job and volunteering with the ACLU and the Legal Aid Society. To me, that shows a lot of character and ambition."

"Ambition nothing, I was exhausted. But I also learned a lot from volunteering."

He thought for a moment. "I'm going to tell you something that I've never admitted to anyone." He glanced over at her to reassure himself. "The first four years at Harvard, I did the typical spring break things, traveled abroad during the summer, screwed off like the rest of my friends. When I started law school, my father told me I had to start spending break times at the firm, sort of like an intern. I resented it. I figured I'd be working my ass off soon enough. He knew how I felt, but he didn't say anything.

"That first week during Christmas break I showed up like I was supposed to. I was given a small office, and I mean small. In fact, now it's that storage closet the admins use."

Mia issued a short laugh. "Seriously?"

"Oh, yeah. I couldn't believe it, especially since there were a couple of empty offices with windows."

"I can see your dad trying to teach you a lesson."

"He never said a word about it, and I didn't, either. I thought, screw him. I wouldn't give him the satisfaction of complaining. It took me a couple of years, but I figured out that he'd saved me a lot of grief. Ended up, respect was more important to me than being the boss's son. It never would have mattered how good an attorney I was if I hadn't earned my place in the firm."

She stayed quiet for so long that he finally took his gaze off the road to look at her. Had he revealed too much?

Her lips curved in a soft smile. "Thank you for

sharing that with me." She touched his face, innocently enough, but he tensed, because with Mia, there was no innocent touch. It was crazy how easily she got to him. "You missed a spot." She circled the side of his jaw with the tip of her finger and then moved her hand to the tightness at the back of his neck.

"Good thing it's a straight shot to Diamond Head, or we'd be lost already," he murmured.

"Oh, am I distracting you? Sorry," she said, with a sly smile in her voice. "I'll try to keep my hands to myself." She folded them primly in her lap, then slowly, deliberately crossed one shapely leg over the other, effectively snaring his attention.

So that was how it was going to go down. Him trying to put on the brakes, and her doing all she could to make him crack.

5

THEY SKIPPED THE scenic lookout where several groups of people were already stationed, and chose a spot off to the right. Mia inched closer to the edge of the cliff and stared down at the waves slamming the jagged black volcanic rock below. She'd long given up on trying to tame her thick, unruly hair. Between riding with the top down and the stiff breezes that swept off the ocean, the best she could do was keep it secured in a ponytail so that her hair wasn't whipped into her face.

"Look at those two." With her chin, she indicated a couple who'd left the lookout and were picking their way down toward the water.

"Did you want to go down for a closer look?"

The words were no sooner out of David's mouth when water shot out from the blowhole, jetting a good twenty feet into the air. The scene was spectacular, the white spray fanning out in every direction. Though they stood a safe distance away, Mia reflexively leaned back and bumped into David. The adventurous pair below shrieked and scrambled backward, trying to avoid getting wet. Or worse.

Mia shuddered. "The view from here is just fine, thank you."

He casually slipped an arm around her shoulders, and she sighed and relaxed against him. His skin was warm on hers, his scent spicy and all male.

"Yeah, I wouldn't get too close," he said closer to her ear. "Apparently the spray is unpredictable. There's an underground lava tube that extends into the sea and when the waves crash into it, pressure builds inside the tube. The water can shoot up to thirty feet. Certainly enough to knock someone over."

Mia pulled away to look at him, disappointment pricking at the pleasure of being held. She'd had the impression this trip had been a last-minute decision. That he'd pulled it together for her. "How do you know all this stuff?"

"I read a few guidebooks."

"When?"

"Last night."

She frowned. "You were in a rush to leave my room so you could read guidebooks?"

His mouth twisted wryly. "Right."

She was instantly sorry for bringing up last night, especially when he lowered his arm and they were no longer touching. Did he think he was rushing her? "I wouldn't have minded if you stayed," she said finally.

He kept silent for too long as he faced the ocean. That his sunglasses hid his eyes meant nothing—David was an expert at masking his emotions. "I know, and I wanted to stay."

"But?"

Sighing, he rubbed the back of his neck. "I was trying to give you some time."

"You've been doing that for nearly three years."

"This isn't the same."

Mia hated that she couldn't read him. Hated it even more that he had the ability to shut everything out, including her. She stared at his familiar profile, her gaze taking in the proud strong chin, the perfect nose, the sculpted jawline. He was from Pearson stock all right, cultured, reserved, confident.

Maybe what she'd seen at work was all she'd get. Maybe she'd been wrong to think there was another David beneath the layers of breeding that prevented him from being more human.

But then there was last night. That kiss.

No, she wasn't wrong.

At the memory of his hot, wet mouth covering hers, his tongue plunging in and taking no prisoner, her insides fluttered. He hadn't been guarded then or reserved. Definitely confident though. He'd be that way when he made love to her.

Damn him, he made her want more. She wanted him naked and sweaty and vulnerable, all of his defenses gone. She wanted him inside her.

She hesitated, but just for a second. "Remember," she said, "I don't work for you anymore."

He'd straightened, suddenly alert. "Look." He slid his arm around her shoulders again, brought his cheek close to hers and pointed.

Her first reaction was annoyance that he'd ignored her comment, or was trying to distract her. Not that she disapproved of his methods. She snuggled a bit closer and squinted in the direction of his outstretched arm. "What am I looking for? I see some kind of boat—"

"No, to the right. Farther out. Just watch."

She stood still, barely able to think about anything but his slightly beard-roughened cheek pressed against her skin.

"There." He hugged her. "Did you see?"

"Only for a second. What was it?"

"I'm pretty sure it's a whale. Let's keep watching. It might surface again."

Her gaze transfixed on the spot, she waited, thrumming with excitement. Their patience paid off. In a matter of seconds, not one but two animals arched out of the sea, making their mark with a jettison of water that echoed the blowhole.

She gasped. "Wow."

"We're lucky. I read that this was a good spot for whale watching, but only in the winter. This is the tail end of the season for them to be passing through."

The reminder that he'd wasted last night reading nearly threatened her improved mood, but she decided she wouldn't allow it. They *were* going to talk, but perhaps this wasn't the place. For now she planned on enjoying the fact that he still held her and that she could feel the steady beat of his heart against her arm.

"I see something else," she said, keeping her sights on the horizon. "It almost looks like another island. Is that possible?"

"Yep." He didn't move, which suited her fine. "I see it, too. When it's clear enough they say you can see any one of three other islands—the Big Island of Hawaii, Lanai and I can't pronounce the last one. Starts with an *M*."

"I know. These names are crazy. I have no idea how to pronounce the highway we're on."

"You mean Kalanianaole?" he asked smugly.

"Like I would know if that's right or not. That sounded pretty good, though. What's up with that?"

"I cheated. I listened to the vocal part of the GPS directions earlier."

"Sly, Pearson, very sly." She turned enough to rest a palm on his chest, then tilted her head back and gazed up at him, daring him to kiss her.

A tiny twitch at the corner of his mouth was the only reaction she got. But for him, that was something. In his dark glasses, she saw her reflection, saw what a mess her hair was, and sighed.

He nudged her chin up a fraction. "What's the matter?"

"I just caught my reflection in your glasses. My hair. Yikes."

He gave her ponytail a light tug. "I like your hair. Especially when it's down." His warm moist breath bathed her cheeks, made her heart skip a beat. "You used to start out with it down when you came to work in the morning. It would still be damp."

She was blown away that he'd noticed that minor detail. It seemed he'd barely spared her a glance unless they were working together on a case. "Your hair would be slightly damp, too, sometimes."

"Mia, I want—" He closed his mouth, gave his head a small self-deprecating shake. "We'd better get on the road. We have a lot more to see."

She stopped him from drawing away. "David, please."

"Look, you're only here for a week, you've made plans with your friends, and here I am butting in."

"That's not what you were going to say."

"No," he admitted, clearly conflicted about something. "This is more complicated than I anticipated."

"This? You mean, us?"

He nodded.

Mia didn't try hiding her frustration. "We're in Hawaii. I don't work for you anymore. We're obviously attracted to each other. What's complicated about that? It's only one week, David, and then we go back to our respective lives."

He flinched slightly, something she'd never expected. Had she hit a nerve? Was he worried that she'd want more from him than he was willing to give? His life was already full, between work and social obligations that went with being a Pearson. If the rumors were true, his mother not only fixed him up with dinner companions to attend company functions, but family gatherings, as well.

A sudden and truly awful thought struck Mia.

"We both know what I'm going back to," David said, his voice bringing her out of her dark thoughts. "But what about you? What's life going to be like for you now that you've left the firm? Shelby mentioned something about a business?"

This time, she drew back and focused on the waves that had gotten choppy, spewing whitecaps toward the rocky shore. There was one huge reason why he'd be hesitant to engage in no-strings sex.

Without looking at him, she asked, "Are you seeing someone?"

"What? Jesus, no." He made a sound of disgust. "Of course not. Where did that come from?"

"I figured that's why you'd backed off last night. Why you seem kind of skittish."

He snorted. "Skittish?"

"Poor choice of word maybe, but I'm pretty sure you know what I mean."

"Come here."

At the way his voice lowered to that sexy rasp, she sucked in a breath and shot him a sidelong glance. Her heart started to race as she slowly swiveled back toward him. Taking her hand, he drew her close. His arms went around her, and he locked his hands at the small of her back. She was certain he was about to kiss her. Instead, he moved his mouth near her ear.

"If I told you what I want to do to that body of yours," he whispered, his jaw grazing her sensitive skin, "you'd run as far and as fast as those long sexy legs could carry you."

Her brain went numb. She had no clever retort. The rest of her body sprang to life, blazed with excitement. There was no place for her arms except to loop them around his neck. Leaning into him, she felt the beginning of his arousal.

He took her lobe between his teeth, nibbling lightly, and then briefly pressed the flesh between his lips before nuzzling the side of her neck.

A stiff wind whipped off the sea and buffeted them. Already mentally off balance, Mia pressed her entire body against him, trying to steady herself. He was broad and solid, so much more than she would have guessed a week ago. With a deep inward sigh, she relaxed her hand and dragged her palm over the contour of chest muscle beneath the green tennis shirt.

"Ah, Mia," he murmured against her warm skin.

There were still people using the lookout, cars whizzing past them on the highway. Did he even remember where they were? Did she care? How could she? This was David. This was what she wanted.

Her lips parted, and he pushed his tongue inside, kissing her with a sweeping thoroughness that made her forget everything.

They broke apart only when a noisy minivan full of children pulled off the highway and parked not far from their rental. David straightened and finger combed his hair. Feeling like a guilty teenager who'd been caught making out, Mia tugged at the hem of her shorts and adjusted the front of her blue tank top. It didn't seem to matter that she wore a bra. Her nipples were tight and hard and testing the elasticity of the fabric.

"We should go," she said, averting her eyes so that she didn't have to meet with the white-haired van driver's disapproval.

"Just a minute," he said, concentrating on something on the horizon.

She swung her gaze toward the open sea. "Another whale?"

David noisily cleared his throat, sounding as if he were trying not to laugh.

"Oh." She spotted the problem. They really were going to have to do something about that swelling.

They waited until the gang was clear of the van and headed for the lookout before David used the remote to unlock the BMW's doors.

"Where to next?" she asked breathlessly.

He stuck the key into the ignition. "You have a swimsuit under that?"

"I do." She had on bottoms, anyway.

"Good." He exhaled a long breath. "Maybe we can find someplace to cool off."

So much for staying in public to prevent him from stripping off her clothes and kissing every inch of her. David mentally shook his head as he guided the car onto the highway. He hadn't checked the GPS but he already knew that as long as he stayed on the coastal road they wouldn't get lost.

He was acting like a damn kid, unable to curb his libido. Hell, he had more pride and self-control than to put himself—or Mia—on display. In fact, he took pride in his self-control. How messed up was that? And acting the way he had in front of a carload of children? He wasn't himself. He was never reckless. It didn't matter that no one here knew him. That wasn't the point. He knew. Worse, Mia knew.

"Why are you scowling?"

He tossed her a glance, noticed the gaping neckline of her top, and gripped the steering wheel tighter. "I'm sorry about back there."

"I'm not."

He shook his head. "That was inappropriate."

"Wait," she said. "I want to be clear. Do you feel that way because somebody saw us, or because it's me you were making out with?"

He cringed at the term. "Both."

She made a low growling sound. "You do not get to say that. Not after that kiss last night, or for that matter, after what you whispered to me earlier."

"I know. I know. I'm sorry for all of it."

"First, I'm pretty sure you're speeding," she said, and he checked. She was right.

He eased his foot off the accelerator, even more irritated now. The highway was starting to wind, and he had no business being distracted from his driving. Having Mia sitting beside him was dangerous enough.

"Second, you're here in Hawaii, not at work. You've already shown your hand. You can't run hot and cold on me. It's not fair."

He smirked at that. She was inarguably right. Her impeccable logic was part of what made her a good lawyer. "I didn't think I should jump your bones without taking you out on a date first."

Mia chuckled. "Okay, now we're getting somewhere." She sighed. "For God's sake, I hope today qualifies as a date."

He cocked a brow at her. "This is an interesting new side to you."

She laid a hand on his thigh, close to his crotch. "Back at you."

He hissed in a breath. If she was waiting for a comeback, she'd be disappointed. She hadn't actually put her hand where he'd like it, but his body reacted anyway. "Um, for the sake of our well-being, I think you might want to keep all your body parts on your side of the car while I'm driving."

"So, pull over." She chuckled again, sounding completely satisfied with herself as she tucked her hand into her lap, wiggled around—more to drive him crazy, he suspected, than to get comfortable—and laid her head back against the headrest. "I'm ready for a swim."

"So am I," he muttered, and steered them off onto a turnout. "So am I."

She quickly straightened, her lips parting in surprise, her eyebrows arching above her sunglasses as she stared at him through the dark lenses. Good. She thought he'd called her bluff.

Ignoring her and trying to quash a smile, he consulted the GPS.

"Are we lost?" she asked.

"Nope. I think there's a beach nearby where it's not too rocky to swim." He turned on the GPS's audio, and they listened to the voice pronounce the odd-sounding Hawaiian street names. "Did you get that?" he asked.

Mia started laughing. "If you're counting on me, we're never going to get back to Waikiki."

Her cheeks and nose were pink, and although he'd applied sunscreen earlier, he figured he probably had gotten too much sun himself. He reached over to the glove box, his arm grazing her breasts in the tight confines of the car. Hearing her sharp intake of breath, he smiled to himself.

"Here." He tossed her the tube. "You can use some on your face and shoulders."

She squirted the white cream onto her palm, then removed her glasses and slathered the sunscreen on her face, shoulders and arms. Looking over at him, the sun shining in her face, her green eyes so beautiful, they sparkled like emeralds, robbing him of oxygen. "You, too," she said, her gaze lowering to his mouth and lingering. "Take off your sunglasses."

She waited for him to do as she asked, then squeezed more sunscreen into her palm. Using her fingertips, she smoothed the cream across his chin, dabbed it over his cheeks and down to the tip of his nose.

"Thanks." He rubbed in the leftover white spot on her chin.

"I'm not done with you," she said in a throaty voice that got to him in a not so surprising way. "Look down."

He frowned, automatically glanced at his fly, then smiled to himself when she applied the sunscreen to his exposed nape. When she was finished, he asked, "Done with me now?"

"Not even a little."

He looked up. Their unguarded eyes met. Something so primal stirred inside him that he didn't know what to do.

She was wrong about one thing. He hadn't shown his entire hand. He hadn't told her the firm wanted her back, and that he'd been ordered to do anything to make that happen.

But he'd been wrong, as well. Wrong not to tell her up front. He knew what he had to do. He didn't like it, and didn't much like himself for agreeing to do it. But his feelings changed nothing. The firm needed her.

6

THEY STOPPED BRIEFLY at Sandy Beach, aptly named because the rocks were fewer and a long stretch of white sand left plenty of room for sunbathers, picnickers and children building sandcastles. The problem was there were too many people for David's taste, and even if there weren't, the waves were too big for a pleasant swim or any other water activity that interested him.

A few people rode surfboards and kept safely to the left of the swimmers and kids using boogie boards. He and Mia mutually decided to move on.

Makapuu was the next beach, different than Sandy in that it was a bay surrounded by rocky cliffs that kept it somewhat hidden. Again, the main drawback was the number of people, mostly bodysurfers testing their skills against the powerful waves, or the spectators sunning themselves.

"Let's stop for a while," Mia suggested just as he was about to pull onto the highway again.

Although David preferred going elsewhere, he cut the engine. "No swimming here. The way the waves break in the middle of the bay makes it too dangerous. That's why there are only bodysurfers in the water."

"I do want to swim, but I'd like to have a better look at the bay and those two islands out there. Wish we had binoculars."

He squinted at the pair of barren islands not too far from the coast. "Not much to see. One of them is called Rabbit Island. No rabbits left, though. It's a seabird sanctuary now."

She grinned at him. "You're just a fountain of information. Did you get any sleep at all last night?"

"Not much," he muttered, as he watched her get out of the car, the hem of her shorts riding up high enough that he caught a glimpse of her peach-colored swimsuit. Grudgingly he climbed out behind her. "I'm thirsty. Supposedly there's a small town about ten minutes from here."

She smiled over her shoulder at him. "I just want a quick peek. I doubt I'll ever make it out here again."

He stood alongside her, their shoulders almost touching. "You mean to this side of the island?"

"No, Hawaii."

"Too many other places on your list?"

"I wish. More like too much work and no time for anything else. Not to mention no money," she added ruefully. "This is kind of a last hurrah."

"Ah, the business Shelby mentioned." After he'd returned to his room last night, he'd belatedly wished he'd asked questions during dinner with Shelby as a buffer. Find out if their new venture would be a further complication for him. "I understand now why you felt you had to leave us," he said casually. "With the hours you worked, starting up a business would have been nearly impossible."

"Nearly?" She chuckled. "Not a chance I could have done both effectively."

"I didn't catch what kind of business it is."

"Sort of a concierge service."

He waited for her to elaborate, and when she didn't he said, "Good thing you have a PR person."

"Look at you being all funny." Mia gave him a wry smile. "If I thought I could nab Pearson and Stern as a customer, I'd be all over it. We're going to rent out everything from power tools for that small one-time do-it-yourself project to designer handbags in case you want to impress your future in-laws."

"I'll keep that in mind."

"Or if you need a wife for the day, we'll provide that, too."

He choked out a laugh. "Pardon me?"

Mia's teasing grin made her eyes sparkle. "To do errands or plan or help host a party, that sort of thing. Our sorority held a fundraiser when I was in college, and Shelby, Lindsey and I rented ourselves out for a day. That's how we came up with the idea. But we never had the seed money until now."

"Should I even ask what service you rendered?"

"Oh, just use your imagination."

"Right." That could get him in trouble. "So I assume the new firm you're going to work for is smaller and won't swallow up your time."

She looked startled. But when she said, "I don't want to talk about work or anything related," he understood. She looped an arm through his and leaned her head on his shoulder. "This week will go by fast enough."

Briefly closing his eyes, he deeply inhaled the exotic scent of her spicy shampoo. His initial instinct had been right. Maybe it was wrong to tell her about the offer now and ruin her vacation.

This was insane. He'd never in his life been this indecisive. Or cowardly.

No, business would wait. For once, he was putting himself and Mia first.

"Come on. Let's get out of here."

MIA HAD DONE THE RIGHT THING. She'd spent enough sleepless nights expounding on the pros and cons of quitting the firm. If her decision disappointed David, then too bad. No "if" about it. A third-generation lawyer like him wouldn't understand that she simply didn't want to practice law. Neither would her family and her former coworkers. That's why she'd withheld that small detail. She couldn't help it if everyone assumed the new business was a sideline. Eventually she'd have to tell her parents and siblings, but she figured the shock would be easier to overcome once Anything Goes was a success.

She finished off the last of her ice-cold strawberry slushy just as they found Bellows Beach Park. Unlike the other beaches, there were trees. Lots of them, providing both shade and privacy. Fortunately, there weren't many people there: a small group of surfers, a few teenagers who probably should've been in school. But that was it, and the white sand seemed to go on forever, which meant they weren't likely to be bothered by newcomers.

They easily found a secluded spot where someone had recently been camping, if the charred remains of a small cook fire were any indication. Nearby, palm fronds had been used to erect a makeshift shelter. The lean-to wasn't much, probably helped to block the breeze, but it also provided privacy. Privacy she had no intention of wasting.

She glanced over at David, who'd just cut the engine, and found him watching her. Was he thinking the same thing? "I wish I had thought to bring a beach towel from the hotel," she said, "or picked up a couple of those straw mats I saw people using."

He gave her an amused smile.

"What?"

"Did you enjoy that slushy?"

"I did. You can't say I didn't offer— Oh, crap." With a swipe of her tongue, she'd figured out why he was still smiling and pulled down the visor. In the mirror, she regarded her clownish reflection with a sigh. "You could've said something earlier."

"I shouldn't have said anything at all. It'll fade soon enough." The way his voice dropped told her he had the same idea about how to use their lucky spot.

She dabbed ineffectively at the red stain that made her lips look as if they were twice as big as they were. "How did I manage to do this?"

"Fortunately I love strawberry." He leaned over and kissed her briefly before sweeping his tongue across her lower lip. "Hmm, very good."

"I dare you to do that again."

"Plan on it." He winked and opened his door.

She *really* wished they'd done more kissing before he got out, but she quickly changed her mind when he stepped out of the car, removed his sunglasses and yanked up the hem of his shirt. After exposing his flat belly, he paused to unfasten another button at his neck before pulling his shirt off altogether.

Mia blatantly stared. It was rude. Definitely embarrassing because she couldn't quite close her mouth. And she didn't give a damn. He had a gorgeous chest, tanned and lightly muscled. But how? He worked all the time.

"I'm not stripping," he said. "Not here. No matter how much you beg."

"Even if I get on all fours?"

He gave her a long, studied look. "You get down there, and I'm sure we could come to some kind of agreement."

"Oh, wow, if the ladies in the office could hear you now."

A flush tinged his cheeks. "What happens in Hawaii stays in Hawaii, remember?"

"I'm just saying…" She opened her door and slid out, unable to drag away her gaze. "How do you have time to go to a gym?"

"I don't." He shrugged. "I have a few routines I do at home every morning to keep in shape for tennis."

"Plus, you're tan." She narrowed her eyes. "It's March. You used a tanning bed."

"Right," he said dryly. "I had to be in Florida recently." He stuck his head inside the car, and fiddled around, the fluid movement of his shoulder muscles holding her gaze prisoner. "Do you play tennis?"

"Badly." She was dying to ask what he'd been doing there, why he hadn't been home licking his wounds because Friday had been her last day. Obviously it wasn't all business that had taken him south, or he would've had no time for the outdoors.

She heard the trunk pop, and met him at the rear of the car to see what he had stashed.

There were a pair of folded blue beach towels and two rolled-up straw mats that seemed to be a favorite of tourists crowding Waikiki beach.

"Should have bought a cooler and drinks." He grabbed the towels, passed them to her and then got the mats.

"I'm impressed you thought to bring these, although not surprised. You're thorough, if nothing else."

He closed the trunk and pocketed the keys, watching her the whole time, a wicked glint of amusement in his brown eyes. "Yes, I am, I'm thorough in everything I do."

Somehow the amusement melted into a promise that made her skin tingle with yearning. If this were a dream, she'd be hitting the snooze button, loath to wake up. Good God, this was David. In Hawaii. With her. Sure, she'd known him for a long time, but that was some other David, who in some ways she'd gotten to know quite well.

This version brought back the old feelings she'd struggled with early on, day after day.

"Why are you staring at me like that?" He rubbed her upper arm, as if she were a child that needed soothing.

"Like what?"

He frowned, the tender concern in his eyes nearly her undoing. "As if you're afraid."

"That's crazy. What's there to be afraid of?"

His mouth curved into a thin smile. "I hope not me."

She sucked in a breath when she realized he was right. Fear had tucked itself in a small corner of her heart. But that wasn't on him. It would be her own fault if she tried to make more of this week than it was. "Nope. I just want to have a good time, no regrets, no expectations."

"I want that, too."

"Perfect." So why did his agreement hurt a little? Now that she'd had a small taste of him, was she getting soft? Getting greedy? She had to stick to her cheesecake rule. She could only indulge when she ate out. Not even a sliver was allowed to reside in her refrigerator since one bite was impossible for her. It invariably led to a minibinge.

Thinking something might come of this week would be a mistake. If David had seriously wanted to pursue her for a real relationship, he could've done that in New York. No, she'd seen the women his family deemed appropriate, and while she was no slouch, she wasn't on anyone's social radar. Now that she wasn't even going to practice law, she could just imagine his parents' horror. But that was good, right? All she wanted was a one-week fling—that's what this trip had been about from the beginning. That it was with David didn't change the game.

His hand closed over hers, and she snapped out of her musings. "We don't have to stay," he said quietly. "Say the word, and I'll take you back to the hotel."

"No, I'm having a great time. I spaced out, I know." She shrugged. "Sorry. It's just that— Nope, not talking about work."

"No argument here." He let go of her hand, and used the car to balance himself while he kicked off his deck shoes.

"Mind opening the trunk again? I want to leave my purse and sandals."

He did as she asked, then frowned at the peach-colored bikini top she pulled out of her bag.

"It's my top," she said.

"I know." He glanced at her breasts. "Where are you going to change?"

"Here."

He didn't seem thrilled with the idea, but then he didn't have a say. He squinted through the trees at the pair of figures walking close to the water at the south end, far enough away that their genders were undistinguishable. "I saw a sign for the restrooms about a mile back."

"It'll take two seconds." She reached under the tank top and unsnapped her bra. "You can warn me if anyone's coming."

"Okay," he said, doubt reflected in every syllable of the word.

She smirked. "You do have to turn around."

"Right." He surveyed the area once again before he slowly gave her his back. "You might feel more comfortable changing in the car."

"It's a convertible."

"I meant that I'd put the top up," he said dryly.

"Okay. All done. You can turn around."

He wasted no time in doing just that. His gaze went unerringly to her breasts, which were barely covered by two skimpy triangles of fabric. The way they were thrust out while she tied the bow in back made her a bit self-conscious. Made her clumsy. The task seemed to take forever.

He finally dragged his gaze away, looking slightly embarrassed.

She nervously busied herself with wiggling out of her shorts, being careful not to pull the bikini bottoms down with them. Then she took her time folding everything, trying to get rid of the jitters.

After depositing her clothes in the trunk beside her bag, she did a quick check of her front to make sure everything was in place. She cringed when she noticed a spot on her upper thigh she'd missed covering with the bronzing lotion. Unfortunately, she also noticed the slight roundness of her belly because she never made time for the gym, nor had she done crunches in forever.

Sighing, she gathered the towels she'd set aside while she changed, and strategically held them up in front of her. Only then did she realize that David had slipped out of his khakis to reveal a pair of red swim trunks. His thighs were nicely muscled, though not overly so, but his calves surprised her with their bulk and definition. They didn't belong to a casual jogger, but more like a serious runner.

He closed the trunk, and they followed a grassy path through a cluster of trees that bordered the pristine white sand. There was no need for discussion as to where they'd plant themselves. They stopped at a spot that was half-sunny, half-shaded, and shielded them from the north side of the beach by the leafy lean-to.

David untied the straw mats, and then shook out each one, placing them side by side, so close together they almost touched.

Mia dropped a beach towel on each mat before focusing her gaze on the water gently lapping the shore.

She was painfully aware that David was staring at her. It was weird that she would feel more self-conscious in a bikini than being naked. But then, this was full, unforgiving sunlight. Not the same as a dimly lit hotel room. On the upside, she got to eye him, too. She looked over at him.

He gave her a guilty smile. "I feel like the proverbial kid in the candy store."

She grinned and lowered herself to the mat, positioning herself so that she could lean back, giving the illusion of a flatter tummy. Giving the illusion that she was cool and composed when her insides were doing somersaults.

He got down beside her and tossed the car keys on the mat, and mirrored her position, so that the upper halves of their bodies were both in shade. The sun burned down on their thighs and calves. She stared at the pesky mole near her knee that she'd hated since grade school. Had she been smart, she would've had it removed while she still had health insurance.

"You've been out of law school for eight years now?" she asked, turning to meet his eyes. She was pretty sure he was thirty-three, past the age a lot of guys started getting married. No way she'd bring that up.

"Yep. It feels like twenty." His brows drew together to form a slight crease. "You have the greenest eyes. I used to wonder if you wore contacts to get them that color."

"Maybe I do."

He shook his head.

"How do you know?"

"I've had almost three years to figure it out."

She snorted. "You barely spared me a glance."

"Think so?" A slow, sly smile lifted the corners of his mouth as he looked so deeply into her eyes that her entire body flushed. He leaned over and pressed a gentle kiss to her lips, then touched the corner with the tip of his tongue.

"Oh, God, I still have clown lips, don't I?"

David stopped her inane muttering by kissing her again, this time coaxing her lips apart and kissing her long and hard and deep. She felt herself start to slip backward, and his arm was suddenly behind her, guiding her back until their kiss broke and she was lying supine on the mat and staring up into his warm brown eyes.

"No one's coming," he whispered as he trailed a finger from her chin down between her breasts, his touch so light she couldn't be sure she hadn't imagined it.

He kissed her eyes, kissed her nose, brushed his lips leisurely across hers. Then he touched her breast. She automatically arched up, filling his hand. Her nipples tightened, communicating their need. He found one through the fabric of her top and circled it with the pad of his thumb.

"We shouldn't have stopped," he whispered huskily. "We should've gone straight to the hotel."

"You said no one's coming," she reminded him in a weak voice.

He groaned, and pushed aside one triangle of her top. For a second he just stared at her bared breast, his eyes dark and hungry, and then he put his hot mouth on her puckered flesh. His moist heat bathed her skin, and she shivered, squeezing her eyes closed when his teeth scraped her hard nipple.

She blindly reached for him, found his hip and slid

her hand around to cup his firm, round ass, urging him closer until his erection pressed her thigh. She moved her leg so that she rubbed him just right, smiled when she heard his soft groan, groaned herself when he sucked hard at her nipple.

He cupped her other breast, inched the fabric over until he'd exposed the other nipple. He rolled his tongue over the crown, stopping briefly to nip at the hard tip. But when he simply breathed on it, Mia shivered.

"Do you know how long I've wanted to do this?" David whispered. "How much I want to kiss you everywhere." He kissed the spot between her breasts, and then moved to the heated skin between her ribs. When he got to her navel, she experienced momentary panic and tensed.

She didn't know why. No one was around. But the mood had definitely shifted.

He sighed, and she felt his withdrawal even before he planted a final kiss on her belly. "Come on," he said, his breathing irregular. "I know where we can get some great room service."

7

PEOPLE CROWDED INTO the hotel elevator behind them, and Mia found herself pushed to the opposite corner of the car from David. But with David at six-two and her at five-nine, they could still see each other over most other people's heads.

Or maybe it wasn't such a good thing. All the way through the lobby he'd tried to convince her to go straight to his suite with him. She'd resisted, too hot and sticky and desperately wanting a shower. But had they been alone in the elevator, she had a feeling he might have pulled out all the stops in trying to win his argument.

God, merely thinking about how he touched her with the perfect amount of pressure, kissed her in all the right places, nuzzled her neck exactly where she liked it, was enough to make her give in. Her only viable wall of defense was Lindsey and Shelby. It was almost five, and she'd feel like crap if she didn't at least check in with them.

The elevator dinged, signaling that it was about to stop at the seventh floor and her gaze locked with his.

"One hour," David mouthed, over the head of a short, white-haired lady. "No more."

"Or?" she mouthed with an arched brow.

"I'm coming for you," he said aloud, ignoring the inquisitive looks shooting at him.

Mia pressed her lips together to keep from giggling like a little girl, and hurried off when the elevator doors slid open.

The second she opened the door to her room, her heady rush crashed and burned. Shelby was lounging on the shady balcony, alone, an open book sitting on her lap. It looked as if she might have dozed off because she jerked slightly and then swung her unfocused gaze toward Mia.

"Hi." She straightened and rubbed an eye. "Wow, it's gotten warm out here." She closed the book, rose and stretched. Then she stepped into the room and closed the balcony door behind her. "Mind if I turn up the A/C?"

"Of course not." Mia dropped her small bag and sunglasses on the bamboo secretary, her heart heavy with the possibility that Shelby had spent the day alone. "What did you do today?"

"I went to the beach, walked forever, swam in the pool, found this adorable bikini and matching wrap in the shop next door. Wanna see it?"

"Sure." Mia watched her friend disappear through the open adjoining door, and then slid a peek around the connecting room. "Where's Lindsey?"

"I don't know. I haven't seen her." Shelby reappeared with a bag. Before she opened it, she grinned at Mia. "How was your day with that tall, gorgeous hunk?"

"Great. I wish you'd come with us," Mia said breezily.

"It's like a whole different island once you get past Diamond Head. Totally awesome."

"Uh-huh."

"What?"

Amusement danced in Shelby's hazel eyes. "You seriously think I wanted the 'G' version?"

"Sorry." Mia shrugged, feeling unexpectedly defensive. They weren't kids anymore. She was not going to discuss the intimate details between her and David. "I don't have anything juicy for you."

Shelby's gaze narrowed speculatively, but she wisely dropped the subject. "Check this out," she said, dumping the contents of the bag onto the bed.

There wasn't much to the hot pink bikini. The back consisted of a thong, the legs were cut high and the front dipped into an indecently deep V bordered by a narrow ruffle. The top was a mere token. Of the three of them, Shelby was the only one who could get away with wearing something like that, or for that matter, even consider it.

Shelby arranged the two pieces on the bed and then held up the brief *pareau* cover-up apparently meant to be wrapped low around the hips. "What do you think?"

"You'll probably get arrested."

She laughed. "Hope it's by a male cop."

"You always did like a guy in uniform."

"Hey, you know...I've never dated a police officer."

Mia chuckled, and shook her head in mock disapproval. Since they'd considered the possibility that other guys might respond to their Facebook wall, Mia asked, "Happen to meet anyone?"

"A really cute lifeguard." Shelby sighed. "We're having drinks at sunset tomorrow."

"Great."

"He's built like a god. The guy has to do some serious weightlifting."

"I never knew you to be attracted to that type."

Shelby shrugged, her lips twitching mischievously. "For one night, he'll do just fine."

"God, listen to us." Mia furtively consulted her watch. Only forty-five minutes before she was to meet David. "I'm going to jump in the shower."

Shelby glanced at her watch, too. "I guess I should text Lindsey about tonight. Just to remind her." She wrinkled her nose, looking undecided, then studied Mia. "Frankly, I didn't think you'd remember."

Tonight? Mia frowned, then suddenly recalled it was their birthday night. The time they'd agreed to have a joint celebration for their January, February and March birthdays. "How could I forget that?" she said dismissively, her disappointment so acute she thought she felt her heart sink to her stomach.

She walked to the closet and rifled through the few things she'd hung up, her thoughts going to David. It wasn't as if she couldn't still see him tonight—later, after she'd had dinner with Lindsey and Shelby—but she had to call him, let him know plans had changed. She'd take her cell phone into the bathroom with her, turn on the shower so Shelby couldn't hear and call him. He'd be disappointed; so was she. They'd both get over it.

She took a couple of deep breaths, and yanked a green halter top off the hanger. She'd have to hurry and sneak her cell phone out of her purse while Shelby was busy texting Lindsey. Quietly she closed the closet door, and turned around. Shelby was sitting on the wicker chair beside the dresser, watching her.

Mia jerked. "Damn, you scared me. I thought you were in the other room."

"Before I text Lindsey I wanted to know if you're bringing David."

"No. We planned this weeks ago. Just us girls, remember?"

Shelby grinned. "You're such a bad liar."

"What?"

"Swear to me you remembered about tonight."

Mia hesitated. "I did. I—" She briefly closed her eyes and groaned. Then she stared apologetically at her friend. "I might have confused the days."

Shelby chuckled. "Look, I don't care. We're here, that's celebration enough in my book. And Lindsey, well, she's apparently forgotten, too and I'm not going to be the one to tear her away from Rick."

"Have you seen him?"

"No. You?"

Mia shook her head, and lowered herself to the edge of the bed facing Shelby. "When was the last time you heard from her?"

"This morning."

"A text?" Mia asked, and Shelby nodded. "Me, too."

Shelby sighed dramatically. "Oh, God, Mom, tell me you're not going to get all worried and screw up the evening."

Mia gave her an eye roll, but the truth was, she was a bit concerned. Of the three of them, Lindsey was the most conservative, the most sensible and really good about making sure everyone was accountable. "Okay, one question, does it make sense to you that she wouldn't make sure we knew where she was? Or not here planning every detail for tonight?"

"That's two questions," Shelby muttered crossly and straightened. "Oh, shit, now you've got me worried."

Mia wondered if she should contact David yet. She was going to be late meeting him, that much she knew, but how late? "Honestly, I'm not really worried, more curious."

"You're right. She is being weird."

"Let's text her and ask her about tonight. I'm cancelling. We can choose another night later."

Shelby dug her phone out of her shorts pocket, and her fingers immediately went to work. After she'd sent the text, she sank back and frowned. "I should've called instead."

"That's another weird thing. Lindsey doesn't usually text us as much as she calls."

"True. So why doesn't she want to talk to us?" A grin tugged at Shelby's mouth. "Unless— Did you meet him last time?"

"Nope."

"Me neither. Wonder if she's told him her real name yet?"

"I want to see him," Mia said, getting up and heading for her bag.

Shelby laughed. "Me, too. You gonna call?"

"Yes, ma'am."

"She might not answer."

"Then we both keep calling. Don't leave a message, other than to return the call. You know her, she'll be worried or nosy and won't be able to help herself." Mia withdrew her phone from her bag and stared at it. It wasn't fair to leave David hanging. No matter what happened, she was going to be late. She hadn't even showered yet.

She'd tell him she would be delayed an hour or two, give him a summary version, offer to explain later. He'd be disappointed, but he'd understand.

"SHE'S GOING TO BE so pissed at us." A gleeful grin spread across Shelby's face as she and Mia crossed the lobby in stealth mode, alert for any sign that Lindsey had left the pool and might turn the tables on them.

Shelby wore her new bikini, with the ill-named cover-up tied low around her hips. She looked so stunningly gorgeous with her long tawny hair fluttering in the breeze, that Mia thought she just might hate her a tiny bit.

"Don't look so cheerful," Mia told her. "We have to make this look like a coincidence." She'd left on her swimsuit with the tank top, minus the shorts, as if she were making a casual trip to the pool for a late-afternoon swim.

"Do you think she suspects?" Shelby asked, oblivious to the male heads turning in her direction.

"No way. She didn't say where she was. I could hear the splashing and kids laughing in the background. For all we know she could be at another hotel and the joke will be on us."

"Oh, hell. That would be a bummer."

"Yeah," Mia murmured. Bummer for sure. She could've been with David instead of spying on their too-secretive friend. Part of Mia's motive was plain nosiness, the other part was honest concern. Lindsey was acting strangely about this dude. Twice during their brief conversation, Mia had hinted that she and Shelby wanted to meet Rick. Both times Lindsey had subtly blown them off.

They decided to go the long way from the lobby because it would give them an opportunity to scope out most of the pool area, while there would be little chance that Lindsey could spot them first. A horde of people still wet from the pool or beach were exiting the area as they approached. Made sense since it was close to the dinner hour, but that wasn't going to help their cause.

As soon as Mia spotted the familiar thatched pool-bar roof, she indicated to Shelby that they should head toward the guy signing out beach towels near the restrooms. They both wore sunglasses, but Mia knew that, like herself, Shelby was avidly scanning the groups of guests that remained poolside, lounging on chairs, reading or sipping fruity drinks.

"Oh, my God."

Mia swung a look at Shelby, who'd stopped and was staring in the direction of the giant rock waterfall. One of the boulders threw a portion of the deck into shadow and created a small semiprivate nook. Squinting behind her sunglasses, Mia caught a glimpse of Lindsey's long blond hair. The chaise on which she lounged butted up against another chair occupied by a man, stretched out on his side, facing Lindsey. He had longish sun-streaked brown hair, tied back into a short ponytail.

"Holy crap, check out his tats." Shelby lowered her sunglasses an inch and peered over them.

Mia did the same. She saw one tattoo on his upper arm, another just above his shoulder blade, though she couldn't make out what they were. The rest of him looked pretty good—lean, muscled, broad where he should be—but absolutely, positively not Lindsey's type.

Mia had to take a second glance to make sure the blonde was actually her friend.

"I don't believe this," Shelby said, shooting Mia a stunned look before resuming her openmouthed stare.

They both watched as he leaned toward Lindsey and kissed her. Her hand immediately went to her hair the way it always did when she was nervous. But she didn't pull away.

"I must be hallucinating," Shelby muttered.

Mia blinked just to be sure.

"Would you ladies like a cocktail?"

They both turned to the tall, narrow-faced waitress, who seemed to have appeared out of nowhere.

"Desperately," Shelby said.

"I'm pretty sure you have to be more specific," Mia said absently, and then advised the waitress, "Nothing for me, thanks."

"Make it a Mai Tai— No, wait." Shelby pulled a face. "We need to find a spot to sit. Catch us your next time around, okay?"

"Sure." The waitress shifted her tray, smiled and stalked off to the next guest.

Mia glanced over at Lindsey and saw her friend trying to get the waitress's attention. Mia quickly averted her gaze. "Great," she murmured. "I think Lindsey might have seen us."

Like a pro, Shelby maintained a poker face. "Okay, then let's go get our towels. And then— What?"

"I say we go over and say hi, pretend this is a coincidence. We postponed the birthday dinner. She knows we'd be looking for something else to do. Why not come down for a swim?"

"Right." They walked to the counter and each signed out a towel. "Is she looking this way?" Shelby asked.

"I haven't checked." Mia draped the yellow towel over her arm and slid a furtive look from under her lashes. "Oh, hell."

"Is she looking?"

"I don't know," Mia said, sighing. "But Jeff is here, and he just spotted me."

DAVID HAD BEEN IN THE SHOWER when Mia called his cell phone and left a message. She was going to be late, wasn't sure how long, it had something to do with previous plans with her friends, and she'd explain more later. She'd said she was sorry. Twice. And she'd sounded genuinely disappointed. But that hadn't lessened his own disappointment. Or frustration.

He put on some music while he perused the room service menu, poured himself a scotch and tried to relax. But reading the menu only reminded him that the romantic dinner he'd planned might not pan out. He eyed his phone sitting on the bar, flirted with temptation and finally ordered himself not to call her back. She would've given him the green light had she wanted to talk to him.

Instead, muttering a mild oath, he laid his head back to stare at the textured ceiling. She and her friends had planned this trip together and naturally had their own itinerary. He had no business feeling put out. He knew he was being totally selfish in wanting her to spend every minute with him, but he didn't give a damn. This could be their last chance to see if there was something there between them, figure out if the feelings he'd been suppressing were real.

His restless gaze landed on the crystal desk clock. Only twenty minutes since she'd left the message? How could that be? With the time difference, it was too late to call his office. He sure as hell wasn't about to talk to his father. He'd want to know if David had presented the offer to Mia. Which he would have done by now if he hadn't had a personal agenda.

But damn if he'd feel guilty about that, too. For three years he'd kept on blinders, concentrated on his job, refused to allow the smallest crack in his professional armor where Mia was concerned. It wasn't even just about Mia, although she'd been his ultimate test. For the eight years since he'd been out of law school, he'd always put work first. And yes, of course he was concerned about losing clients and avoiding cutbacks. The possibility of layoffs ate at him, and he was willing to do almost anything to prevent the firm from going that route. But he wouldn't sacrifice a chance with Mia.

He'd forgotten about the scotch he poured, and took a long slow sip, letting the liquid burn all the way down his throat. Thinking about the office wasn't doing him any good. The decision to extend the offer to her at the end of the trip was a good one. The right one. Tonight and the next few days had to be strictly about them.

Ironic, really, that this trip was for both personal and business reasons, after he'd prided himself in keeping those two areas of his life separate.

He inhaled deeply, then exhaled slowly. Of course this whole thing could blow up in his face if she thought his every action since arriving in Hawaii had been about luring her back to the firm and not about wanting her for himself. No, she knew him too well. He had to trust that she held him in higher esteem than to believe him capable of conning her. Mia wasn't just beautiful, she was damn smart.

Smiling, he easily pictured her lying on that crazy straw mat, her dark hair fanned out around her slim shoulders, her green eyes hazy with desire. He loved the way her lips unconsciously parted, ever so slightly, the second before he kissed her, and the way she tasted— cool and sweet and just the right amount of eager.

Well, hell, thinking about her like this and nursing yet another unattended hard-on wasn't doing him any favors, either. Not that he couldn't take care of himself, but he'd only resent her absence all the more.

Abandoning the rest of his scotch, he pushed off the chair. Waiting around the suite was a mistake. He'd have his phone with him in case she called, but he needed to expend some energy, stop doing so much thinking. What he needed was a good swim.

8

"JEFF, PLEASE, LET ME GO. I don't want to get wet." Mia tried to keep her angry voice low and not cause a scene, though luckily, very few people were close to them. But when he tightened his arms around her, his boozy, fetid breath nearly making her gag, she was sorely tempted to kick him in the balls.

"Come on, baby, for old times' sake." He drew her within an inch of the water's edge. "We had us some crazy fun in the pool last time, remember?"

"That wasn't me, you idiot," Mia growled. Thank God Lindsey and Rick had left and weren't witness to this. Shelby was getting a drink. "Now let go, or I will hurt and humiliate you."

Jeff roared with laughter. "I didn't know you were into that stuff. I like it."

Mia poked her elbow back until she made contact with his ribs, and he yelped, momentarily loosening his hold. Sure that had been enough to make her point, she stepped away. He quickly recovered, laughing, and banded his arms around her so tightly that she could barely breathe.

Damn, she didn't want to do the girlie thing and bite him, but if that's what it took…

"Oh, hell, you're gonna make me waste a perfectly good drink, you ass." Shelby stood with one hand on her hip, the other holding a pineapple-and-cherry-garnished drink that she had poised to throw in Jeff's face.

"That won't be necessary."

At the sound of David's deep, rumbling voice, Mia's pulse leaped. Embarrassed more than relieved, she turned her head to look at him. His face was devoid of expression, not so much as a brow moved, but she saw the fury in his dark eyes.

"Hey, David." Jeff blinked blearily at him, oblivious to the unspoken threat. "How's it going?"

"Let go of her." David's chin went up slightly, his jaw tight. His hands stayed relaxed at his sides.

"I was just leaving," Mia said, not wanting to see the situation escalate.

With Jeff distracted, she easily shook away from him and went to stand between David and Shelby.

Jeff frowned, glanced from Mia to David. "Hey, are you two…?"

"Yes." David tersely cut him off, and slid a possessive arm around her.

"Sorry, man." Jeff shrugged, and then set his sights on Shelby, giving her a sloppy lopsided grin.

"Yeah, that'll happen." She snorted out a laugh, and then popped the cherry from her drink into her mouth.

Jeff just shrugged before he jumped into the pool, and the rest of them moved quickly toward the bar to avoid being splashed.

"Just so you know," Mia said to David, "I totally could have taken him."

He gave a grudging smile, telling her he hadn't shaken all his anger. "I should've backed off. I would've liked to have seen that."

She bumped him with her shoulder. "How about I buy my big strong hero a drink?"

He hesitated, glanced briefly at Shelby and moved his arm away from Mia. "I didn't mean to intrude. I only came down for a swim."

"You're not intruding. We were just spying on our friend Lindsey." Shelby shrugged. "We got busted."

Mia pressed her lips together and gave her friend a withering look.

David laughed. "Spying?"

"No, not spying." Mia sniffed. "We hadn't seen her since yesterday and we wanted—"

"To check out the guy she was with." Shelby's eyes sparkled with mischief.

"That's not quite accurate," Mia said.

"And?" David was clearly trying to control a smile. "Did you approve?"

Shelby's light brows knitted. "Surprised the hell out of me. Really cute, but not what I expected." She looked to Mia for confirmation. "Not for Linds."

Mia stared back at her, dumbfounded that she'd speak so freely in front of David. "Okay." She stepped back. "I am going to my room and take a nice long shower. You two—" She waved a hand. "Do whatever."

"Wait." Chuckling, David caught her hand. "I'm going up with you."

Mia hesitated, momentarily meeting Shelby's eyes. She didn't want to ditch her friend.

"Go. Good riddance." Shelby made a shooing motion

with her hand. "You guys are screwing me up. How am
I supposed to get lucky with you hanging around?"

Mia groaned, shook her head.

"Bye-bye," Shelby said, grinning, and then sauntered
away, an exaggerated sway to her hips.

One of David's eyebrows went up as he stared after
her. "She keeps that up and she's going to have more
luck than she can handle."

"She took a hula lesson this afternoon."

"Ah."

"You're drooling."

He took his gaze away from Shelby's retreating back,
and smiled at Mia. "Jealous?"

She coyly toyed with the top button of his tennis shirt.
"Mmm, maybe a little."

"Just so *you* know, I wasn't drooling. At least, not
over Shelby." Ignoring the few remaining guests at the
bar, he slid an arm around her waist, brought her close,
stared at her mouth with an intensity that sent a shiver
of anticipation down her spine. "I think it's time we go
to my suite."

"I still have to shower."

"Just so happens I have one, along with a sunken tub
big enough for two."

"But—"

He nudged her chin up and kissed her. A firm but
leisurely kiss, nothing too risqué or demanding, but still
his boldness surprised her. This spot wasn't like the
beach where trees or cliffs hid them. Here they had an
audience. "Now," he whispered.

DAVID KISSED HER AGAIN as they waited for the elevator,
then kept his distance until the couple who'd followed

them into the car got off on the fourth floor. The doors had barely slid closed when he leaned against the back, taking her with him, spreading his legs and cradling her between his thighs.

"You're crazy," she whispered breathlessly, her lips damp, her eyes glazed.

He took her face between his hands, kissed her deeply and almost didn't hear the elevator signal its approaching stop on the eighteenth floor.

Mia quickly spun around to face the doors as they slid open. A stooped elderly couple, the man walking with the aid of a cane, slowly entered the car. David had immediately straightened, but stayed cautiously behind Mia to hide his aroused state. She moved back, to give the couple room, her bottom intimately bumping him.

David hissed in a sharp breath.

Mia's back went ramrod stiff. She'd clearly figured out the problem and eased away from him. Though not much. Not enough to stop his body from reacting to the snug feel of that sweet, curvy ass.

The white-haired woman considered the numbered panel, peering closely, both through and then over her glasses, while David prayed that the pair would get off on the next floor.

Her gnarled finger hovered a moment, the doors already starting to close. "Is this elevator going down, dear?" she asked, turning to Mia.

The woman blinked, then tilted her head and frowned over her glasses at David as if seeing him for the first time. Her gaze swept Mia's face, and then went back to David, her eyes narrowing in indignation.

He stuck his head out to the right so it wouldn't look

as if he were hiding. "We're going up, ma'am," he said politely, wondering why Mia hadn't answered.

With an air of disgust, the woman abruptly gave them her back. "Harold, we're on the wrong elevator. We need to get off." She stared up at the flashing floor numbers as they ascended.

"So what," the man snapped. "We'll ride the darn thing back down."

The woman stubbornly searched the panel, but by the time she figured out which button to press, they arrived at David's floor. "Excuse us," he said, his hand pressed to Mia's back as they both exited.

He walked them out of view, then stopped to look at Mia. Her face was stained a guilty red, and she looked as if she were ready to explode at any second. They heard the doors sliding close, and she burst out laughing.

"What?"

"That woman—" Mia sniffed, dabbed at her watery eyes, laughed some more. "Did you see her face? I don't know what she thought we were doing."

"We weren't exactly innocent." David couldn't help but join in on the infectious laughter, though he wasn't entirely comfortable that they'd been caught.

"We were only kissing, and not even in front of them."

"Right."

"Oh, David, she didn't *see* you." Mia automatically glanced at his fly.

He said nothing as they continued toward the suite, while digging in his pocket for his key card. It wasn't like him to behave in such an undignified manner. In fact, he'd indulged himself quite a few times today.

Funny, he'd never pictured Mia letting her hair down that way, either.

"You're not upset, are you?"

"No, of course not. No one knows us here." He stopped at his door, opened it and stepped aside for her.

Her brows had drawn together in a slight frown, but as soon as she stepped over the threshold, her pensive mood appeared to vanish. "Whoa. This is some hovel. And what a view."

She seemed to take everything in at once, her gaze sweeping the rich, dark hardwood floors, Oriental rugs, the Hawaiian artwork on the walls. At the sliding glass door to the ocean-side balcony, she paused to stare at the polished dining room table that could accommodate eight diners.

"This place is bigger than my apartment," she said, twisting around to survey the subdued tropical-print sofa and love seat. "I don't even want to know how much this sucker costs for a night."

He snorted. "Trust me, you don't. I only splurged because I haven't taken a vacation in years."

She stepped out onto the balcony, noticed that it wrapped around the corner and laughed with delight. "I could spend the whole week right here and be happy."

He came up behind her, slid his arms around her and nuzzled her neck. "Okay," he murmured against her warm sweet skin.

She laughed softly and leaned back into him, hugging his arms to her waist. "From up here you can see the ocean's different shades of blue," she said in a shaky voice. "You drive me crazy when you kiss my neck like that. But you know that, don't you?"

He smiled. "We can have dinner out here if you want. We should be able to catch part of the sunset."

She turned in his arms to face him, the bewitching green of her eyes knocking the breath out of him. "But then we'd have to hurry our shower."

"Screw dinner," he said, and covered her mouth with his.

Her eager response pleased him, triggered a need in him impossibly greater than he'd experienced on the beach. She pushed against him so hard that he stumbled back a step. She went with him, clutching the front of his shirt, returning his kisses with a fervor that matched his.

But it was no good, her arms shielding her breasts like that. He wanted to feel them pressed against his chest. He wanted to see her perfect round breasts bared again. He needed to see all of her.

With Herculean effort, he pulled away, ignoring her wide startled eyes. "Inside," he said, all but dragging her into the parlor.

He headed straight for the bedroom, unable to tamp down the pressure building inside of him like a volcano ready to explode. This wasn't him, nothing close to who he was or how he behaved with a woman. Normally he was patient, waited for the right mood. He tried to be thoughtful, even romantic at times, designing the right setting—candle, flowers, the whole thing.

But with Mia, he couldn't think straight. Around her it seemed that all he did was react, lose himself in the primal satisfaction of tasting her eager mouth, coaxing her nipples into tight buds flushed dark with arousal. The way he felt was crazy—animalistic—and he couldn't seem to do a damn thing about it.

MIA ENTERED THE BEDROOM ahead of David, both of them ignoring the light switch. The drapes to the balcony door were open halfway, and pinkish gold rays bathed the room in a sensual glow that made her heart lurch. The Asian-inspired armoire and headboard matched the tasteful parlor furniture, and the beautiful tan silk duvet that topped the king-size bed was a far cry from the floral spreads that serviced her economy room.

She was startled to discover that her legs were trembling a little when she turned to face David. Maybe because there was something different about him. Nothing scary or awful, kind of thrilling really. The way he looked as if he were doing everything in his power not to strip her naked and force her back onto the bed.

"David?" Her voice came out strange, husky and tentative.

"I know, Mia," he said quietly, brushing a gentle finger across her lips.

What did he know? She wasn't even sure what she was going to say herself. But when he drew his fingers down the front of her top and then slipped his hand underneath, she said, "Shower first."

"All right." He splayed his fingers across her belly, grazed the underside of her breast through her bikini top.

It wasn't fair that his palm could feel so dry and cool when her skin was fever hot. Nor was it fair the he smelled so clean and masculine.

"Don't."

He met her eyes, his surprised and alarmed. Promptly he let his hand drop. "Mia, I'm sorry."

"No," she said, feeling horrible for giving him the

wrong impression. "No. It's just that you've showered. I haven't."

Relief softened his mouth. "Would it help if I told you that you smell so damn good I want to—"

"No." She put a hand over his mouth, and then laughed when he nipped at her palm. "Don't you dare try to talk me out of it."

He took her by both wrists and stretched her arms over her head.

Her pulse went nuts. He had to feel it. "What are you doing?"

"Helping you undress." He yanked her tank top off before she could respond.

"I doubt that's going to work out well," she said, and gasped when he freed her bikini top and bared her breasts. The cool air danced over her nipples, and she knew without looking that they were fully extended.

He tossed both tops over his shoulder, his gaze captured by her breasts.

Then he hooked his fingers into the elastic of her bikini bottoms.

All rational thought deserted her. The trembling started in her chest and moved down her legs, and there didn't seem to be a damn thing she could do about it.

David was crouched in front of her, urging her to step out of the bottoms, and she braced a hand on his shoulder, praying hard that she wouldn't end up in an embarrassing heap.

He kissed the area just above where her bikini wax ended, and then slowly got to his feet.

At the raw hunger in his eyes, a wave of warm pleasure washed over her. He tenderly touched her breasts, and rubbed the pad of his thumb over one aching nipple.

She swallowed hard, wishing his shirt were off, wishing he were as naked as she was. It would only mean trouble. She really did want that shower before they made love, but right now, like an addict craving a fix, she needed to feel the friction of his bare, muscled chest rubbing her naked breasts.

"Go," he whispered hoarsely.

"Take off your shirt first."

"Go." He gripped her by her upper arms, his fingers digging lightly into her flesh as he held her away from him. The anguished expression on his face should have been enough to keep her at bay, but a part of her was thrilled that she'd undermined this man of iron will. "Now."

She shook free and pushed his shirt up. "Come with me."

"Mia." He hesitated, but only for a second, and then fumbled with the drawstring to his swim trunks, stopping long enough to help her pull off his shirt.

She stepped back, watched him strip off his trunks, barely able to catch her breath. He was hard, really hard, and much bigger than she'd imagined. When he kicked his trunks out of the way, a sudden and totally inappropriate giggle tickled inside her throat.

This was hardly the same man who was always impeccably dressed, never had a hair out of place, or God forbid, tolerated a cluttered desk or office.

He didn't notice her amusement. His gaze roamed her nude body, his lips damp and slightly parted, muscles tensed, like a hungry cougar ready to pounce on his next meal. His attention lingered on the recent wax job, and his small smile seemed just as predatory.

"Shower," she reminded him as she backed up, no longer feeling in control.

"Right direction," he said, "but you're about to ram that cute behind of yours into the door frame."

"Oh."

"You can turn around. I won't bite." Amusement gleamed in his eyes. "Yet."

She lifted her chin, and then her gaze snagged on his twitching penis, and she got all wobbly inside again. When he touched himself, she forgot what she was doing and stared at him, a warm flush of excitement enveloping her entire body. It took her a second to snap out of it. She continued to back up, annoyed when she bumped her hip before crossing the threshold into the bathroom. She patted the inside wall, found the switch and flooded the bathroom with a soft golden light.

The room was huge, lots of glass, brushed silver fixtures, glossy tile and granite. Her gaze went briefly to the big deep whirlpool tub. It would take too long, she promptly decided, and reached for the handle of the glass-enclosed shower.

"Be careful." David was right behind her, his hand touching her back, his thick arousal rubbing her ass, as he reached around to turn on the faucet. "The water gets hot quickly."

She smiled to herself. Who didn't?

9

IT SEEMED AS IF IT TOOK A LIFETIME for the water to adjust to the right temperature. In a small, crazy way, Mia wished that she hadn't coaxed David to join her. She wasn't sure she wanted to have sex for the first time with him while standing up. She could've taken the fastest shower in history, gotten all squeaky clean and been ready for him to do all kinds of delightful, unspeakable things to her in mere minutes.

Not that he was wasting any time while they waited. He pushed aside her hair and kissed the back of her neck, slowly moving his hips so that she could feel his need for her rubbing hot and heavy against her ass. She closed her eyes, totally forgetting where they were for a minute, and then his hands were on her shoulders and he was gently guiding her toward the spray of lukewarm water.

He let her go and, instantly feeling bereft, she turned her head to look at him. He smiled, kissed the tip of her nose, and took the big puffy lavender bath pom-pom off the granite shelf and started soaping it.

"Is that yours?" she asked, surprised.

"No." The affronted face he made was really cute. "It came with the suite. I had it unwrapped and ready just in case."

She grinned. "Just in case?"

"All right, I admit it. I knew I was getting you back here if I had to throw you over my shoulder."

"Ah, you say the sweetest things."

With one dark brow cocked in amusement, he slid the soapy, fragrant pom-pom down her back and over her buttocks, then wedged his hand between her thighs and slowly slid the pom-pom back and forth.

She gasped and turned to face the tiled wall, using it to brace herself. She didn't utter another sound, just closed her eyes and let him glide his hands down her inner thigh to her ankle. He thoroughly washed her calf and then swept up her other calf, causing her to hold her breath when he lingered at her opposite thigh. When he finally moved up higher, it was his hand he used to wash her pussy.

He slid a finger between her lips, and she tensed, then shuddered convulsively.

"Easy, baby," he whispered, slowly withdrawing his finger. "Not yet."

She hadn't come, if that's what he thought. That would be insanely fast, but that she could feel such acute arousal so quickly, that she could come so close to falling off the edge shocked the hell out of her. When he went back to scrubbing her back gently with the pom-pom, she swallowed hard, not sure if she welcomed the delay.

But it became obvious that was his intention, and she willed the quivering in her chest and legs to stop as he finished lathering her arms and shoulders.

"Turn around," he said in a gravelly voice that made it hard for her to move.

He didn't wait, but took her by the shoulders and forced her to face him. His gaze went to her breasts. Hers went to his swollen cock, and she leaned back against the cold tile wall for support. She wanted him inside her. Wanted him with a growing desperation she didn't think herself capable of.

Setting aside the pom-pom, he lathered his hands and then cupped her breasts. She looked at his face, but his lids lowered as he concentrated on torturing her tight, aching nipples. But his lips…God, his lips were damp, the tip of his tongue slowly swiping at his lower lip.

"Kiss me," she whispered.

His gaze leisurely rose to meet hers, one side of his mouth quirking up slightly. "Where?"

"Everywhere."

His nostrils flared, he flexed his jaw. He released her breasts, rinsed his hands and made sure she was soap free, as well. Then he turned off the water and grabbed a big fluffy towel off the rack.

She stepped out of the shower into the waiting towel, and he dried her off, starting with her shoulders and neck, kissing every area he dried as he went down her body. He lingered at her breasts, laving each budded nipple before circling them with the pointed tip of his tongue. She closed her eyes while he nipped and suckled and scraped with his teeth. When he got to her belly, her eyes flew open, but he startled her by not slowing. Instead, he quickly dispensed with the job of drying off the rest of her.

When she reached for the other towel to return the favor, he stopped her. Employing the same towel he'd used on her, he impatiently took on the job himself, making a swift task of it.

He surprised her yet again by slipping his arms around her, hauling her against him and kissing her thoroughly and a bit roughly, all vestiges of his illustrious control crumbling before her.

The thought that she could do that to him thrilled her. She figured it was time to give him a surprise or two, and wrapped her hand around his cock.

He jerked, uttering a guttural sound that was both primal and sexy. His already dark dilated eyes turned the color of midnight, and he stared at her as if she'd somehow betrayed him.

She didn't let up. She stroked downward, and as she came back up, found the moist crown with a sweep of her thumb. Bending to taste him, she was abruptly stopped by his hand threading through her partially damp hair. He grabbed a fistful and pulled her up, and if she hadn't willingly complied, she had a feeling he wouldn't have been gentle. The idea should have appalled her, not thrilled her.

"Wait," he said, his grip on her gradually loosening. He massaged her scalp for a moment, then lifted her chin and kissed her softly on the lips. "You're making me crazy," he whispered against her mouth. "But you know that, don't you?"

"You think I have any sanity left?" she answered breathlessly.

He smiled, his breath coming out in rasps, teasing her sensitive jaw and throat.

"Come here," he said, dragging her with one hand toward the bed and grabbing the duvet with the other.

She got the message and helped him stash the duvet then toss the myriad of decorative pillows onto a green upholstered chair. As soon as the bed was cleared off, they fell onto the sheets in a tangle of arms and legs.

"I sure hope you have condoms," she said, the thought just occurring to her.

"A whole big box." He pushed the hair away from her face and kissed her eyes, her nose, her cheeks, then rolled over and got the condoms out of the nightstand drawer and set the box next to the lamp.

Mia grinned. He wasn't kidding. It was a really big box. "Cocky bastard."

"Confident." He licked one nipple, rolled the other one around with his palm. "Big difference."

She wasn't in any mood to debate. She closed her eyes, and his hand slid to her belly, lower, pausing to trace the outline of her bikini wax as he urged her thighs apart. There was no need to ready her. She was wet and slick, and she vaguely thought to remind him again about a condom. Expecting to feel his hand, she jerked, opened her eyes when she felt his hot breath mingling with her moist heat.

When she looked down, all she saw was the top of his head. He'd forced her legs wider open without her realizing it, and maneuvered himself into position. She sucked in some air and fisted the sheets when his tongue flattened against her, then firmed and pointed to slip between her folds. He instantly found the right spot, jolting her to her core, and she bit back a cry.

She wanted to stop him. He was too good with his mouth, too precise with his tongue. She wanted them to come together. She did. But she couldn't quite make him stop, either.

As the pressure mounted, instinctively she shoved at his shoulders. He wouldn't let up. She squirmed, moaned, shoved some more, startled a minute later to discover she'd cupped her hands behind his head to urge him on.

The tremors started. Dizzying sensations shimmered through her body as the convulsion started slowly, built and built until she shattered.

He brought his head up in the middle of it, quickly sheathed himself, looming over her as he pulled her legs around his hips. He pushed into her with one deep thrust that had her bucking up to meet him. She moaned, met his next thrust by wrapping her thighs around his hips as tight as she could. He didn't stop until she begged for mercy.

MIA YAWNED AND STRETCHED, smiled when David tightened his arm around her naked waist. He lay flat on his stomach, his face buried against the side of her breast. She didn't think he was fully awake yet, kind of caught in the twilight between sleep and alertness, and she didn't want to disturb him. Neither of them had slept much.

She kept as still as possible and stared out at the clear blue morning sky. They hadn't bothered to draw the drapes. Apart from the breathtaking view, being on the top floor facing the ocean had its advantages.

Neither of the past two days seemed completely real yet. In fact, no part of her life seemed real at this point. She still hadn't accepted the idea that come Monday morning, she wouldn't be waking up at five-fifteen, donning a suit and running for the subway to make it to the office before seven. She wouldn't be seeing David, either, as she had almost every Monday for the past three years. It didn't matter that there would be no rules or ethical barrier to prevent them from seeing each other. His life was the firm, hers would be swallowed whole by Anything Goes.

It wasn't even a matter of choice on her part. The business had to succeed. It was her responsibility to make that happen after pushing hard for the idea, after convincing Lindsey and Shelby to quit their jobs. She owed them big-time.

Mia looked down at his dark, mussed-up hair, his broad muscled shoulders. How easy it had been a day or two ago to dismiss this week as a fling. No sweat, she'd reasoned. She'd been out to have a good time, a last hurrah before burying herself in work. David had blown her plans to smithereens.

God, she should have known better. Why hadn't she summoned enough good sense to run the other way? Deep down she probably had known one encounter would propel her headlong into trouble, but the temptation of him had been impossible to resist.

Silly that she'd been reluctant to have sex for the first time in the shower. How on earth had she ever thought it would only be sex? Last night they'd made love.

"'Morning," he murmured, and kissed the side of her breast.

His rough chin tickled, and she giggled. "'Morning back."

He lifted his head, and smiled down at her. "What's funny?"

She touched his face. "I've never seen you anything but clean shaven."

"You've never seen me on Sundays. I rarely shave," he said, rubbing his jaw and eyeing the spot on her breast where he'd kissed her. His gaze moved to her hardened nipple, and his face seemed to transform in a second.

Desire burned in his eyes, and he did that thing with his tongue, where the tip peeked out and dampened the center of his lower lip.

"You've got to be kidding," she said with a laugh.

"What?"

She shook her head, and curled up on her side, facing him, her thighs clamped together.

He sank back down on his pillow with a hangdog expression. "I only wanted to fool around a little."

"A little?" she asked, surprised to find that she was a bit sore. "Think we'd stop at a little?"

"I'll have you know, I have an iron will."

"Uh-huh. I'm pretty sure you lost your right to that claim last night." She caught the glint of lust and determination in his eyes just before he reached for her.

"Whose fault is that?" he asked as he wedged his knee between her thighs.

She got the giggles again. "Stop it. Right now."

"Or else?"

"Or else—" She jumped as his hand slid between her legs and accurately hit its mark. "No fair," she responded weakly.

"Tough." His mouth curved in a devilish smile as he moved in to kiss her.

She lightly bit his lower lip.

"Ouch." He ran his tongue over the abused area. "That hurt."

She knew that was a lie. "Tough."

"Okay," he said, nodding with challenge in his eyes. "You want to play rough?"

She let out a yelp and pulled the covers over her head.

He dove in after her.

DAVID FELT BADLY when he finally got it that Mia was really sore. Last night he'd been in too much of a haze to keep track of how many times they'd made love, but when he checked the box, he found there were four condoms missing.

Four times in fourteen hours. Hell, he hadn't known he still had it in him. Worse, he wanted her again. But as he'd watched her wince as she got out of bed, his conscience quelled the notion. Though he couldn't ease the absurd pride he felt, knowing that he was the first man she'd been with in a very long time.

She'd admitted as much—almost as an apology— when she begged off to take a soothing warm bath and made him promise not to bother her for at least a half hour. As much as he needed a shower himself, he wanted to give her privacy.

Coffee. That's what he wanted right now. A big pot of very strong black coffee. He yawned, rubbed his gritty eyes. Ah, hell, it was almost ten-thirty. They should probably eat, too, they'd missed dinner altogether.

He picked up the phone, thought briefly about knocking on the bathroom door to get her order, but after three years of watching her trying secretly to stash candy bars in her desk drawer, he knew she had a sweet tooth. If she didn't like what he ordered, they'd get something else.

Room service answered promptly and took his order

of coffee, orange juice, eggs Benedict and an assortment of pastries. The poor woman tried to narrow down his definition of *assortment*, but he basically told her to bring anything that was on the breakfast menu and made with sugar.

After hanging up, he moved to the patio door to look out over the ocean, stopping short of stepping onto the balcony. He didn't have a stitch on and had no desire to flash anyone. Sailboats glided across the calm water a fair distance from shore, where small waves broke gently to lap at the sand. Waikiki beach was perfect for swimming, appealing to both young and old.

To the east toward Diamond Head, a dozen or so surfers took advantage of the moderate waves. Beginners, probably. He wondered if Mia wanted to give surfing a try, although he still had quite a list of recommended sights to see on the island.

He turned around and eyed the wrecked bed, the sheets one big snarl of silk, pillows everywhere. No, they weren't going to make it through half the list at this rate, and damned if he cared. He picked up the pillows and smoothed out the sheets, trying to restore some kind of order. Room service would deliver their breakfast to the dining room through the parlor, but he didn't want the housekeeping staff to have to face this mess.

Mia's tank top and bikini bottoms were on the floor near the door, but he had no idea where the rest of her clothes—or his, for that matter—had landed. He looked under the duvet and found his swim trunks. The whereabouts of his shirt was still a mystery when his cell phone rang. He had no trouble locating it because he'd had the good sense to park it in its charger last night.

He had a strong hunch as to who was calling and

warily eyed the illuminated caller display. As he suspected, it was his father. David scrubbed a weary hand down his face. He didn't want to answer. He had nothing to report yet, and admittedly, didn't even want to think about having to talk to Mia about returning to the firm.

Aware his father wouldn't give up just because his call went to voice mail, David picked up the phone. While extending his greeting, he paced toward the bathroom door, listening to make sure Mia hadn't cut short her bath.

The pleasantries were brief. "Well, son, any news for us?"

David massaged the tension at the back of his neck. "Not yet."

A pause, and then his father asked, "Have you talked to her at all?"

"I've only been here two days."

"But you've seen her."

"Yes."

His father's lengthy silence was fraught with questions, possibly an accusation. "I hope you understand how important it is to the firm that we bank this new client."

David's patience slipped. "How can you say that to me?"

"You're right, of course." His father paused again and sighed heavily, and David pictured him pinching the bridge of his nose, frustrated and annoyed that he wasn't in control of the situation. "How's the weather there?"

David smiled. "Fine. Just fine. Look, I'll talk to her. At the right time. You have to trust me on this."

"Of course I do, son. I apologize if I seem overbearing. It's just that it's been rather tense around here lately. Peter sent out the memo yesterday regarding our decision to curtail a number of the usual amenities and the employees are beginning to ask questions. Rightfully so, but we don't have answers. No sense in further sounding the alarm."

Guilt sliced deep. He could explain that her plans for starting a new business made getting her back more complicated, but that would aggravate rather than alleviate his father's worries. Besides, that wouldn't be the entire reason behind David's stalling. "I agree" was all he could bring himself to say, especially when he didn't agree one bit. But he knew better than to try to dissuade his father from being more forthcoming with the employees. The word *layoff* wasn't in his father's vocabulary.

"Well, I guess that's it then."

"How is Mother? Everything well with her?"

"Fine, fine. She's at the Club having cocktails with Gwendolyn Mears, as we speak. Naturally I haven't burdened her with this unfortunate situation."

"No, that would be unnecessary." David smiled thinly. His parents were of a different generation, all right. His thoughts went to Mia. It wouldn't be like that with them. They'd share everything, the good and the bad. She was smart, intuitive, eager to jump in and problem-solve. He'd relied on her opinion many times; he was certain he would again.

The unbidden idea of them as a couple building a life together shocked him, but what surprised him even more was that the thought dug in to him and wouldn't let go. Longing stirred deep and fierce inside him, derailing his thoughts as they spiraled into a vortex of uncertainty and fear. He'd known for a while that she was special, and he'd long suspected there could be something big between them, but this was different, this was serious…

"David?"

He gulped in air, exhaled shakily. "Yes, sorry. I'd ordered room service. I thought I heard them knocking."

"You should go. I have nothing more." Another pause. "Before we hang up, anything I should know?"

David cleared his throat. "Everything is under control."

They hung up, and he stood motionless for a good minute, staring out at the endless sea. He finally tossed the cell phone on the nightstand and took a shuddering breath. Then he turned and saw Mia standing outside the bathroom, bundled in the thick white courtesy robe, her gaze curious. Or was that suspicion?

10

DAVID DID A QUICK MENTAL REPLAY of the end of his phone conversation and decided he hadn't said anything detrimental. He blinked away his guilt, determined that neither his father nor his responsibility to the firm was going to steal this moment away from him. Then he saw her wet, with straight hair, and her skin—devoid of makeup—was smooth and dewy. But it was her startlingly emerald-green eyes that got him every time.

"Is everything okay?" Mia cinched the belt of her robe, her gaze lowering to his bare chest, to his belly, to his cock. She moistened her lips.

That's all it took for him to start getting hard. "Don't worry, you're safe," he said. "Room service is on their way so I won't be jumping you. At least not in the next hour."

Her smile didn't reach her eyes. "You have to go back, don't you?"

He'd started for the bathroom to grab the other robe, but he stopped, frowning. "Go back?"

"To New York. The phone call, I thought—" She shrugged sheepishly. "I wasn't listening. I just walked out here, but from the look on your face I was sure your vacation had been cut short."

"No, it was my father, but—" He took her hand and pulled her close to press a light kiss to her lips. "It was nothing. I'm not going anywhere."

"Good." She looped her arms around his neck and moved her hips against him.

"Ah, being brave because you know we're about to be interrupted."

Her smile was real this time. "Uh-huh."

"You underestimate me." He jerked the robe's belt free.

She let out a shriek of laughter, gathered the lapels together and backed away. "I need coffee. I need food. I seriously need to recover. Have mercy."

"I'd rather have Mia."

"Funny."

A gap in the robe exposed the tempting curve of her right breast, and he had to hold very still. So much for his grand plan to take it slowly. "I have time for a quick shower. Room service will come to the parlor door. Do me a favor and sign for it, please?"

"I'll listen for them," she said, and gave him a pat on his ass as he turned for the bathroom.

David chuckled and shot her a warning look before he closed the door behind him. Too late he realized he should've brought clean clothes in with him. The other robe hung on the back of the door, but he wanted to be dressed and ready to hit the road as soon as they were done eating breakfast. It would be too easy to crawl back into bed with her.

He doubted she'd resist, and her being sore wasn't the issue—he knew how to please her without burying himself inside of her. But that's not how he wanted to spend the rest of their time together. Every minute counted. Once he presented the firm's offer, their relationship had to be on stable ground.

After turning on the shower, he fiddled with the spray control and waited for the temperature to be just right before he got in. He lifted his face to the jetting water. The force was harsh and stung his skin, but he left it alone. The punishment was mild, he decided, but with any luck, strong enough to wash away his lingering guilt.

BY THE TIME THEY HAD EATEN, gotten dressed and Mia had touched base with Shelby and Lindsey, it was already early afternoon. Although David had planned an outing to the north shore of the island via a picnic and swim at Waimea Falls, Mia nixed the idea in favor of sticking closer to Waikiki. She was worn out, feeling lazy and really curious why David seemed determined to fill their every waking hour with a planned activity.

When she suggested taking a long walk down the beach and then finding an outside bar to have a drink, he'd immediately countered with a proposal to first visit 'Iolani Palace and the Bishop Museum, both relatively short drives from the hotel. She agreed, and actually enjoyed the outing, especially the tour of 'Iolani Palace, the only true royal palace used as a residence by a reigning monarch and standing on American soil.

Naturally David opted for the guided tour, which she admitted was informative and fascinating, but as soon as the tour ended and they left the palace, he was ready to hop in the car and head for the Bishop Museum. She put on the brakes, grabbing his hand and forcing him to sit beside her on a shaded stone bench.

"You do realize that you're the kind of person who gives us New Yorkers a bad name," she told him, dismayed that he immediately slipped his sunglasses out of his pocket and slid them on. God, she didn't want to believe that he regretted their lovemaking, and really, there was little evidence that he did—he'd even held her hand most of the afternoon—but still, a surprising jolt of insecurity hit her hard.

"What do you mean?"

"Rushing around like you have a million deadlines."

He smiled ruefully. "I wouldn't call it rushing. Didn't you enjoy the tour?"

"Yes, but I wouldn't mind kicking back, too. We have stressful jobs. Well, *you* do. I did." She sighed, hating that she was getting flustered. But something didn't feel right between them.

She'd noticed the change in him after his shower. They'd talked some during breakfast, but he'd hurried through that, too, claiming he wanted to leave so that housekeeping could clean the suite. It was almost as if he didn't want to be alone with her, or have too much free time to talk. Was he worried that she expected they'd spend every night together? Or that she'd monopolize his time? Maybe she should've begged off doing anything with him today and given him some space.

It took a while, as if his mind was working on overdrive, but he finally responded. "Sounds to me like you have regrets."

"What?" Her heart thudded. "About last night?"

"No." He reared his head back, his furrowed brows

reflecting his bewilderment. "No, I meant about quitting the firm."

"How did you get that idea?"

His lips lifted in a weary smile. "Guess we're both too exhausted to make much sense."

She frowned, trying to think back on what she'd said. Recalling her rambling, she returned the tired smile. "I'm still trying to wrap my brain around the fact that I won't be showing up at the office on Monday. Even worse, how much unchartered, scary territory lays ahead of me." She wished she hadn't admitted the scary part, but it was already out there.

"You're going to do great," he said, closing his hand on hers and giving it a reassuring squeeze. "I've seen you in action. You put your mind to something and it's a done deal."

"Yeah, I've always been pretty goal-oriented." She made a show of unnecessarily shading her eyes, and then took her dark glasses out of her purse and hid behind them. "I'll have zero life, but I'll make the business work."

He barely reacted, only moved his shoulder ambiguously. "Didn't you just tell me you didn't have one before?"

She swallowed the disappointment that rose in her throat. "True," she said lightly, mentally chiding herself. What had she expected? For him to declare that he'd be filling her evenings with romantic dinners and tangled sheets? Nothing would change once they returned. Not only did she already know that, but it's what she wanted. What had to be. With their schedules, there could be no happy medium.

Oh, she knew they could grab a quickie now and then, but after last night, the thought was a bit painful.

"You're quiet," he said, using his thumb to trace an idle pattern against her palm.

"Just enjoying the warm breeze and flowers. Can you believe it's still March?" She abruptly stood. "Come on. Let's go back to the hotel and walk on the beach."

There it was again. At the suggestion, he'd immediately tensed. But why?

"What about the Bishop Museum?" he asked, slowly getting to his feet. "We have only four full days left and a lot more to see."

"Really?" Whether it was his unconvincing tone of voice or the way he defensively jerked one shoulder, she didn't buy it. "You're that interested in the history and culture of the state?"

He heaved a heartfelt sigh. "No."

"Then what?"

Mirroring her frustration, he said, "I don't want you to think that all I want from you is sex."

He hadn't seen the older couple wearing matching loud Hawaiian shirts approach from behind him. As if they'd overheard, they exchanged knowing smiles and, holding hands, veered toward the next bench.

Mia pursed her lips, trying not to laugh, but it turned out it wasn't hard to sober. Something about the couple's shared smiles and the familiar way they touched stirred a wistfulness in Mia's chest that took her by surprise. She looked away from them, unsettled, because she hadn't known she craved that closeness, the kind bred only by years of talking and touching and waking up together in the same bed. *Not now, for God's sake.*

Shaking his head, David groaned, and then gave a resigned chuckle.

Mia pulled herself together, looped an arm through his and steered them in the direction of the car. "Uh, excuse me, Mr. Pearson, but were you there last night?" He only smiled, patiently waited for her to zing him. "I'm pretty sure my participation was rather enthusiastic."

"What I meant was that I don't want you to think that is the only reason why I came to Hawaii."

"To get laid?" She spoke quietly so no one could hear her teasing. "Come on, if that were true, it would have been a lot cheaper to find a date in Manhattan."

David abruptly stopped, forced her to face him. He wore the most awful expression, part angry, part offended.

"Hey, I was only teasing."

He slowly removed his sunglasses, making her wait as if she were a recalcitrant child and he, the long-suffering teacher struggling to compose himself before he meted out suitable punishment. "Look, *Ms. Butterfield*, let's be clear." He startled her by plucking off her sunglasses, too.

She blinked at the unexpected glare, then swallowed at the spellbinding intensity in his brown eyes as they met hers and held on.

He touched her cheek. "I came here because of you, and only you. I won't lie, the sex was phenomenal. That's part of the problem." He smiled a little. "We need to stay the hell away from the hotel and private beaches or anywhere else where I can get away with stripping you naked and doing wicked things to you, or there is no question how the rest of this week is going to end up."

His seductive words and the dark lusty gleam in his

eyes made her body feel all warm and tingly, and her mouth go dry. Not the same predicament down south. She unconsciously squeezed her thighs together as if that would make a difference. If he wanted to get down to business right now in the convertible parked off a busy Honolulu street, she had a nasty suspicion she'd let him.

He studied her face. "You have nothing to say?"

She moistened her parched lips. "I'm still trying to figure out why, exactly, that would be a problem?"

"Jesus." He briefly closed his eyes. "Come on," he said, taking her by the arm. He was already getting hard. She could see the evidence building behind his fly.

"Where are we going?" she asked, all innocence. "The Bishop Museum?"

His smoldering gaze was all the response she needed.

THE BALCONY OFF the suite's bedroom was the perfect spot for watching the sunset. No matter how clear the day had been, a handful of clouds always seemed to gather over the horizon in time to turn the sky a vivid rainbow of pinks and oranges and salmons.

Mia lazily stretched her bare legs out to the railing as she turned to watch David, who was sitting beside her, digging the macadamia nuts out of his vanilla ice cream.

"Are you going to eat that or play with it?"

"What are you, my mother?"

She laughed. "I'm jealous. I finished mine five minutes ago."

He paused long enough to cock a wary brow at her. "I'm not sharing."

"You would if I asked nicely," she said in a sweet voice.

"Of course I would, so of course you wouldn't." He popped one of the nuts into his mouth for emphasis.

"Why *are* you doing that?" She'd watched the same ritual yesterday and it drove her crazy. "It's not as though you're not going to end up eating everything anyway."

"I know."

"So?"

"Cheap therapy. It calms me."

Mia rolled her eyes. "That's what you said about having sex three times in two hours."

He grinned. "That works, too."

She shook her head in mock disapproval and settled back to enjoy the sunset and let him finish his ice cream. After their talk at 'Iolani Palace two days ago, the frantic pace had ended, and every minute had been sheer bliss. It didn't matter if they were simply walking along the beach or making love or picking out that ridiculous souvenir for Annabelle on the couch, or just sitting here as they were now, eating ice cream as the sun dipped. It was all good. Perfect even. Better. Mia couldn't recall a time she'd felt more content.

"Here."

She turned her head to look at him. He held a spoonful of ice cream to her lips. She grinned. "Sucker."

He ate the last bite himself, and then set the empty foam cup next to hers on the small side table. "When it comes to you…"

That he was so serious, so matter-of-fact, made Mia's pulse flutter. "I was teasing," she said lamely.

He smiled, stretched back on his lounge chair

and locked his hands behind his head. "What time is dinner?"

"Dinner?" She frowned, scrambling to figure out what she'd missed. "Oh, the birthday dinner. You were still in the shower when I talked to Lindsey and Shelby this morning. Sorry I forgot to tell you, but we canceled it altogether."

"Why? I thought it was tradition."

"Not canceled, really. We postponed again."

"Hope I didn't have anything to do with it." He seemed troubled by the prospect.

Which she totally adored about him. A lot of guys would've selfishly tried to manipulate her into feeling guilty for deserting them for an evening. "Nope. We decided to wait until we go back to New York." She shrugged. "Shelby's birthday isn't until next week."

"But yours was January twenty-ninth."

"And Lindsey's was on February twenty-fifth." Mia paused, narrowing her gaze on him. "How did you know when mine was?"

"Must've heard people wishing you a happy birthday."

"No way. The admin staff celebrate with cakes or lunches out, but the attorneys—even us baby attorneys—never make a big deal out of our birthdays."

He shrugged, laid his head back and stared at the sunset. A slow smile curved his mouth. "I might have looked it up."

Mia laughed. "I didn't get flowers. Oh, wait. You just wanted to know my sign."

"Your sign?" He swung his leg onto her lounge chair and used his bare toes to torture the sole of her foot.

"Stop it," she said giggling. Damn it, he knew how

ticklish she was there. "Hey, I'm an Aquarian, which means payback's a bitch." She kicked his foot away. "Just so you know."

"Hmm, I didn't know that about Aquarians," he said, laughing.

"You apparently don't know anything about them. I lied. If anything, we're loyal to a fault."

"Okay, what else do the cards say about you?" He jerked his chair closer, and she quickly protected her feet.

"No cards. We're talking about astrological signs."

"Sorry I got my occults mixed up."

"Fine." She sniffed. "Mock me, but you'd be surprised at the accuracy of the descriptions."

"What surprises me is that you follow that stuff."

"It's not as if I read my daily horoscope. I was a kid when I learned about what the different signs mean. Naturally I was curious about mine and if the description applied to me."

"Obviously it did, hence your interest. Tell me about it."

"So you can make fun of me some more?"

Smiling, he reached over to rub her arm. "No, I won't. Now I'm curious."

She eyed him for a moment. "I'm supposed to be outgoing, amiable, highly organized," she said, and he nodded. "I'm always thinking, both a good and bad thing I've discovered. Aquarians are also humanitarians." She tried not to smile as she waited for his reaction.

He snorted. "I'll vouch for that one. You racked up more pro bono hours than any three associates combined."

"So you've reminded me, more than once as I recall. But you never said no."

"You also clocked more billable hours than the rest, and you never once let our paying clients suffer. I couldn't justify saying no." His eyes went flat, and he turned to stare at the sunset. "Your leaving is a major loss for the firm."

She'd been unprepared for the sudden change in his mood. Nice that he acknowledged her professional value, but had he forgotten that the only reason they were here now was because she was no longer an employee?

Mia cleared her throat. "I'm not sure what to say to that. Thanks, I guess."

He stretched his neck to one side, and then the other, staying silent for too long. Then he sighed and looked over at her. His smile wasn't off, not by much, but she could see it. "Tell me more about your sign."

Back to neutral territory. She could live with that. "Of course there are some gray areas. I'm supposed to be objective and not swayed by emotion."

"You don't think that's true?"

"Legally speaking, I can be very objective, but personally, not so much." Instantly she wished she could recall the admission. She hadn't meant to share that much. An hour ago, maybe it would've been all right, but she hated the way the old David was looking at her with those unreadable eyes. The mask was firmly in place, not a hint of emotion revealed.

She turned away, shrugged, tried to shake off her resentment. "I'm also supposed to be happiest when I have a goal, which is completely accurate. I'm looking forward to the challenge of Anything Goes."

His leg was still on her chaise, and he moved his foot

to stroke her calf. "I know it won't be easy, getting the business off the ground," he said, "but I admire the hell out of you for going after your dream like this. Still, it's nice that you have the side job."

It took a second to realize he meant his assumption about her working for a smaller firm. Damn, she wished he hadn't brought that up. How long could she get away with lying by omission? It shouldn't make any difference. This wasn't a romance, it was a week of fun. So why hadn't she told him the truth?

Puzzled and a little sad, she tried to pull together a smile, but she knew it would only ring false. It was time to stop playing games.

11

DAVID STARED AT HER in total astonishment. She'd quit practicing law? He had to have misunderstood. She was the smartest, most promising attorney Pearson and Stern had hired in nearly a decade. "I thought you got a position at a smaller, less demanding firm."

"I know you did." She nibbled at her lower lip. "I'm thirsty," she said, nudging his leg aside and rising from the chaise. "There still should be a couple of colas in the fridge. Want one?"

"Mia, wait." He saw that she had no intention of humoring him, so he followed her into the bedroom, through the parlor to the wet bar. "Why did you want me to think you were working for another firm?"

"I didn't." She took a long time poking around the small refrigerator before producing two cans. "You assumed, and I didn't correct you. It seemed like a good idea at the time."

Shit. His gut clenched. This was bad. For him. For Mia. But he couldn't overreact. For someone who was supposed to be quick on his feet, he couldn't think of a damn thing to say.

"I know you're disappointed." She handed him an ice cold can. Funny, he thought he was too numb to feel it. "I'm sure I've disappointed a lot of people, not the least of whom will be my parents. They won't understand how I could go through three tough years of law school and pay all that tuition, and then walk away." She pressed the can to her flushed face. "Can we not talk about this right now?"

So she hadn't told her parents yet. Interesting. He took the can from her and set it beside his on the bar. Then he sat on one of the tall stools with his legs spread and pulled her close. "You have better instincts than almost anyone I know. That quality is part of what's made you such a damn good lawyer." He lifted her chin when she tried to stare at her toes, and saw her eyes fill with glassy confusion. "Only you know what's right for you. I support your decision." Even as he uttered the words, panic rose in his throat. He forced a smile. "Not that you asked."

"Oh, David." She threw her arms around him and hugged him tight. "That means a lot," she said, her voice a broken whisper as she buried her face against his neck. "Thank you."

He closed his eyes, stroked her back, kissed her hair. Her shoulders trembled slightly, and he knew she was fighting back tears. She was a strong woman. It couldn't be easy for her to become so emotional, and all he wanted to do was ease the hurt and suffering she'd experienced in reaching her life-altering decision. As incomprehensible as it was that she could throw away such a promising career, he meant what he'd told her. He did support her.

He had no choice. Damn it, he loved her, he realized

with a sinking sensation at total odds with the discovery. Probably had loved her for longer than he cared to admit.

Now what the fuck was he going to tell his father?

MIA LET HIM SLOWLY UNDRESS HER. She closed her eyes and deeply breathed in his warm, masculine scent as he stopped to kiss the shoulder he'd exposed and then the top of each breast as he drew the cotton sundress down her body. She felt drained from finally confessing the truth, and doubted she had the energy to do much more than slip between the sheets. Until it had become clear the discussion was inevitable, she hadn't fully appreciated how frightened she was that the truth would disappoint him, make him think less of her.

She'd never dreamed he would be this accepting. It wasn't as if she hadn't seen the shock on his face. Or the pleading denial in his eyes, the moment of hope that he'd misunderstood. For someone like David, who lived and breathed every intricacy of the law, she'd been convinced it would be impossible for him to understand her decision. Smiling to herself, she realized that was absolutely true. He could make no logical sense of it, probably thought she was certifiable, but that made his acceptance all the sweeter.

With a start, she saw that he'd stripped off his clothes—she was already naked—and he was trying to pick her up. "What are you doing?" she asked, although she figured it out a second later.

She grinned, but ended up gasping when he swept her off the floor and into his arms. The trip to the bed was only a few feet, and she smiled when he laid her atop the sheets. She threaded her fingers through his hair and pulled him down for a quick kiss. "Why did you do that?"

He sat at the edge of the bed and massaged her scalp. "You look wiped out." He shrugged, a teasing smile tugging at the corners of his mouth. "I wanted to be your big, strong hero."

Mia laughed.

He feigned a pout. "Ouch."

"Ah, let me kiss it and make it better." She curled up and put her lips to the crown of his penis.

He jerked. "Hey."

"You're complaining?"

He looked serious. "Yeah, I am. I'm supposed to be taking care of you," he said, despite the fact his cock was already hardening. He glanced down, his mouth twisting wryly. "I can't do anything about that."

Mia tried to keep a straight face, remembering something her brothers used to tease each other about. "Maybe if you think about going blind and getting hairy palms?"

David smiled, touched her hair and the tip of her chin, then lightly dragged the pads of his fingers down between her breasts. But it was the tenderness in his eyes that sobered her. Warmth flushed her body, and if she had to speak she didn't think she could do it. Her mouth was too dry, her tongue felt like a lead weight. It took her a few seconds to figure out the frightening pressure in her chest was from holding her breath.

Without warning he rose. She was about to plead for him to stay when he gently nudged her to move over, and stretched out beside her. He lay on his back and slid a comforting arm around her as he urged her to lay her cheek on his chest. She snuggled close, and rested a palm on one of his flat, brown nipples, which firmed beneath her touch. She smiled when she saw that his arousal had not yet subsided. Not for a second did she doubt that she could tempt him into making love to her, but for now it was nice just to be held.

Annabelle was never going to believe this. David. Here in Hawaii. When Mia filled her in it would be the "G" version, of course.

Mia had no idea where the thought had come from, and she didn't even know when the older woman would return from her trip. No, in a way it made sense she'd think about Annabelle now, weird as it seemed. Their talks in the park had always been soothing, a balm to Mia's confused senses, and right now, she couldn't begin to explain the serenity she felt.

Listening to the steady rhythm of his heartbeat against her ear, she closed her eyes, drowsy from the heat, the comfort of his closeness, the awe of his unconditional acceptance. When he skimmed a hand down her back, over the curve of her hip, then lightly cupped her bottom, she felt a stir of excitement in her belly.

She lifted her head and moved her hand away from his chest.

His gaze narrowed. "Where are you going?"

"Nowhere." Pointing the tip of her tongue, she touched it to his already hard nipple.

He tensed. "I thought you were tired."

"I was." She kissed the warm skin right below. "Evidently big, strong heroes get me hot." She moved her mouth to his lean, taut belly, pressed a kiss there. Used her tongue to circle his navel, smiled when he sucked in his stomach.

When her exploration took her too near to his swelling

penis, he curled up, took her by both arms and dragged her mouth to his. "I want to be inside you," he whispered, his voice raw with emotion.

The intensity of it made her tremble as she automatically reached for the box of condoms on the opposite nightstand. She kept her face averted because it terrified her to witness his expression. This man, who was an expert at hiding any hint of feeling, had never sounded more vulnerable.

She tore the packet open and assumed the task of sheathing him, keeping her focus on what she was doing, knowing that he watched her, that his eyes could tell her more than she might want to acknowledge. Already on sensory overload, she refused to look up, even as she felt the weight of his gaze willing her to do so.

He put both hands on either side of her waist and lifted her up until she straddled him. She still managed to avoid his eyes—instead her gaze rested on the curve of his mouth. The smile was different than any he'd given her before, gentle yet unnervingly determined.

He touched her, found that she was wet, lingered there, teasing her, then entered her with two long, lean fingers. She quivered, let her eyes briefly close and pressed against him.

"No, inside," he murmured, low in his throat, and withdrew. He urged her into position, his cock poised to accept her as she slid onto him, slowly, taking him in gradually.

The hands that cupped her hips shook, and his face tensed. She clenched her muscles around him, and he threw back his head, the veins on his neck pronounced.

"One day," he said, his voice thin and raspy, "we

won't need condoms." And then he thrust into her, his reference to the future knocking her emotionally off balance.

A DAY LATER, Mia sat beside David, five rows from the stage, watching the hula dancers use their hands and hips to tell the story of ill-fated lovers. Great. Mia's favorite topic lately. She slumped in her seat, and ordered herself to enjoy the performance.

When David had suggested they visit the Polynesian Cultural Center on the other side of the island, she hadn't balked. Not just because they'd had quite a bit of lazy beach time, but she knew it was going to be a tough day. It was their last full day in Hawaii, and she didn't want to have too much time to think and get all mopey.

Her overactive mind had become her enemy. She still found it difficult to comprehend how graciously he'd accepted her decision to give up her law career.

Maybe he figured her disillusionment was temporary, and she'd eventually come around. There was no way to know, and she'd only make herself crazy second-guessing his reaction. One thing she did know for sure was that something was off. He was a bit quieter yesterday and today, more introspective. But so was she as the time to leave got closer.

And then there was the remark about not needing a condom one day. Yet something else to keep the wheels spinning out of control. So far she'd settled on two interpretations. One was strictly clinical, the other meant that he was thinking in terms of the long haul. Either possibility suggested that he planned to continue their affair in New York. But then again, he hadn't said a word to that end.

It shouldn't bother her since she'd already decided there would be no room in her life for a man. Except this wasn't any man. This was David. It all seemed so unfair—

Oh, God, she really had to get over herself. No, it wasn't fair. The timing was awful and who knew what she'd have done if she'd even guessed. But this was her reality, and the sooner she stopped the nonsense about fairness, the better. She had right now, and she'd be a damn fool not to enjoy it to the fullest.

She inhaled deeply, delighted with the perfumed air, and let her breath out slowly. By the time she repeated the relaxation technique she'd learned during her first court appearance, the song ended and a new set of dancers took the stage, accompanied by the heart-pounding primal beating of native drums. Three very fit, half-naked, brown-skinned Polynesian men using their open palms on the drums had pulled her back to the present.

But it was the swift movement of the Tahitian dancers' hips that had her leaning forward and staring in awe. "Good grief, they look as if they've been plugged in."

"I thought you'd fallen asleep."

"I might have been nodding off a bit during the hula dancing," she lied. Then she cast David an accusing glance. "Guess who's to blame for keeping me up most of the night."

A smile of pure male satisfaction curved his mouth. "I didn't hear you complaining."

She bit back a grin and glanced around to make sure no one had overheard them. There were about two hundred people in the audience, but the drums were loud and everyone's attention seemed to be glued to the dancers.

"I wish we could've talked Shelby into coming with us," she said, knowing that was a half truth.

As soon as the sun had gone down and the torches were lit, everything about the place seemed to change. By day, the cultural center, with its simulated tropical villages and authentic arts and craft demonstrations, was both educational and entertaining. But now that she'd started to relax, sitting in the dimness of the half-open pavilion, the warm air scented by a panoply of flowering trees that grew profusely around the grounds, she had to admit that the setting was very romantic.

He slid an arm around her shoulders, and she gladly leaned against him. "We can bring her tomorrow if you like. We only got to see half the attractions."

She pulled away to look at him. "Did you forget we leave tomorrow?"

"How could I?" He seemed to stare sightlessly at the dancers for a few moments, and then captured her gaze. "What if we stay an extra day?"

The unexpected suggestion was like a splash of cold water in her face. "How? I mean, we both have to get back. There are deadlines—"

"Understood."

She shook her head. "I don't see how it's possible."

"It is if we—"

Someone from behind shushed them. Rightfully so. Mia sent the woman a smile of apology, and turned back to stare at the dancers, her thoughts tumbling even more wildly than they had earlier.

When it finally occurred to her that she was oblivious

to what was happening on stage, she whispered, "We should go."

He nodded, and as unobtrusively as possible they slipped out of their seats and hurried to the sidewalk. When they got to a fork, she started to go right, but he took her hand and led her to the left. Within seconds she saw the parking lot.

"I hope you don't mind that I wanted to leave," she said, spotting his rental near the entrance. "I didn't even ask you."

"No, good call. We have about an hour and a half drive back to Waikiki."

"Really? It took that long to get here?"

"Yep," he said. "I guess I should've considered that when I booked the dinner show."

"No, I'm glad we came. It would've been a shame to have missed seeing what we did today."

"Next time we'll have to plan better and come early." The keys were already in his hand, and he used the remote to unlock the doors.

Mia watched him open her door, her pulse leaping, even though she was annoyed. How could he say something like that and still act so casually? Damn him. He couldn't keep alluding to the future and then let the tension hang over them like a threatening rain cloud. Finally she couldn't stand it. "There is no next time. We leave tomorrow."

He flinched, or at least she thought he had. Maybe he was baiting her, trying to force her to make a declaration. Her breath caught at the thought. When the silence got too thick, she slipped by him to get into the car.

David caught her around the waist. His arm snug around her, he bent to kiss her gently but all too briefly.

Then he gave her a tender smile that made her heart catch, and she instantly forgave him. "I'm being an ass," he said. "But I don't want this week to end."

Mia's chest tightened. "I don't, either."

"The difference is, you're not being a baby about it."

"Trust me, inside I am."

"Good." He nuzzled the side of her neck. "So maybe I can talk you into staying one more day."

She sighed. "First off, it would be too expensive to change our tickets."

"I'll take care of that."

"No," she said firmly. "Anyway, it's not only about the money." She snorted ruefully. "Although in my current position, I can't be cavalier about finances, either. Bottom line, we both have full schedules waiting for us back in New York, and that's not going to change."

But this would, she thought, when he hugged her tighter and kissed her hair. She closed her eyes, felt his quickened heartbeat against her breastbone, heard his muffled sigh. He knew she was right. Delaying the inevitable was foolish, but perhaps now was the time to discuss what would happen after they returned. At the thought, her insides coiled into one big knot.

He released her, waited until she was seated and then closed her door. His silence unsettled her.

After he was behind the wheel and started the ignition, in a light, joking tone, she said, "I can't figure out if taking this week off was a good idea or not. I'd almost forgotten that there's more to life than work."

She stared at his unyielding profile, waiting for him to respond. Whether or not he'd figured out she was fishing for a reaction, he said nothing.

AN HOUR AFTER they'd returned to Waikiki, David ordered a bottle of Mia's favorite chardonnay and chocolate-dipped strawberries from room service, while he waited for her to return with clean clothes from her room. This was their last night in Hawaii together. It should have been perfect, full of romance and promises whispered in the dark, velvety night. Instead, he had never felt more conflicted in his entire life.

Pearson and Stern needed her like a baby needed its mother's milk, and Mia wanted nothing more to do with the law. She was totally convinced she'd been on the wrong career path. He couldn't disagree more. How could she have been such a brilliant attorney? Her instincts were spot-on, every time. He'd learned quickly that he didn't have to second-guess her decisions. In that regard, his judgment had nothing to do with his cock.

Naturally, because all of that wasn't complicated enough, he'd fallen in love with her. He wanted her to follow her dream and be happy, but he owed his father and the firm his loyalty. It wasn't just a matter of the practice losing money. Jobs were at stake in a time when every job was critical. So where did that leave him and Mia?

His right hand started to ache. He stared down at it, and found that he'd clenched it into a fist. He opened his hand, flexed his fingers. He wasn't a man who sought answers in violence, but a large part of him wanted to smash every piece of art in the suite. Nice.

After staring at the city lights from the parlor window, he paced restlessly to the bedroom balcony, slowing briefly to grab the drink he'd forgotten he poured off the bar. Maybe if he put on some music he could relax.

Who was he kidding? He wouldn't relax until Mia came back, until she was in his arms. They would have a great night together. He wouldn't ruin it by thinking about work, much less laying the firm's problems on Mia's lap. After he returned to New York, he'd find a way to land the new client without involving Mia. His father would be disappointed at first, but—

He heard her soft knock and smiled. Although he'd given her her own key card, she never used it. He opened the door. She stood there with her small carry-on, her eyes bright. Too bright. Had she been crying? He drew her inside, got rid of the bag and held her face in his hands. They looked deeply into each other's eyes. Once he started kissing her, he couldn't stop.

12

AFTER MISSING THE final boarding call and being summoned by an airline employee, Mia lumbered toward the jetway with the enthusiasm of a woman about to be thrown in the slammer. She had no choice but to get on the plane and join Shelby, who'd boarded earlier, or forgo the flight, and pay a lot of extra money just to be put on a standby list tomorrow.

While the clerk validated Mia's boarding pass, Mia itched to turn around for one last look at David. He'd driven her and Shelby to the airport, even though his flight wouldn't leave for five hours. Mia had begged him not to because it was silly for him to hang around the airport when he could be sitting at the pool bar, but he'd shut her up by kissing her soundly and that was that.

The woman smiled, returned the boarding pass. Mia hesitated. As much as she wanted that last look, she was feeling ridiculously emotional, and wouldn't it be just wonderful if she got all teary. For God's sake, this wasn't a goodbye. Not really. He'd be in New York tomorrow. Poor guy had to take a red-eye flight home, which was the only last-minute seat he could get.

Mia turned one last time, to see him put his cell phone to his ear. He wasn't even looking her way, his concentration fully on the call. Smiling at herself, she kept on going. All that should-I-or-shouldn't-I nonsense for nothing.

Since she was the last passenger, some of the ground crew were right behind her, and she hurried on board. The flight was full, and she peered down the aisle toward the middle of the plane, searching for Shelby. Due to David's failed effort to get on Mia's flight, she already knew it would be a shoulder-to-shoulder ride to Dallas, where she and Shelby each had to catch separate connecting flights since Shelby had to go back to Houston for two days.

Just as Mia started to pay attention to seat numbers, Shelby put up her hand to get her attention, and bless her, she'd left the aisle seat for Mia.

"Hey, I thought for sure you were going to miss the flight," Shelby said, as Mia opened two overhead bins and, not surprisingly, found them full.

"I almost did. They were about to page the first person on standby." Mia shut the bin, and sighed, eyeing the vacancy under the seat in front of hers.

Shelby drew up her much shorter legs and indicated the empty spot in front of her. "Put your carry-on there."

"You sure?"

"It won't bother me. You'll never have room for your legs."

"Thanks." Mia stowed her stuff, sat down and buckled up.

"Well, obviously David couldn't exchange his ticket. Sorry."

Mia shrugged. "He was even willing to give up his first-class seat, but both our flights were oversold, with long standby lists. And then, the real kicker, we finally realized he'd flown with a different carrier."

Shelby chuckled. "Yeah, that would be a problem. Oh, well, it's not like he's staying and you're leaving. You'll see him when he gets back."

Mia inhaled deeply.

"Right?"

She shrugged. "Yep, he said he'd call."

"Okay, there is something hugely wrong with this picture." Shelby twisted in her seat so that she faced Mia. "An hour ago you two were all over each other, now this act of indifference. Which, by the way, I don't buy for a second."

"We weren't all over each other," Mia said crisply, though she should've known better than to let her guard down and not act as if everything were perfect. She didn't need a barrage of questions from Shelby.

Her friend settled back. "You know I would've given my seat to him," she said, "but the movers will be at my apartment early tomorrow morning, and I have to be there."

Feeling guilty, Mia smiled. "Then you'll drive to New York the day after."

"Yep, I'm still bringing my car. I know it's probably crazy, and who knows, I may end up getting rid of it. Hey, did you get another text from Lindsey?"

"No, but I assume she booked another flight before she canceled today's." Lindsey was staying a few days longer, which initially pissed off Mia, until she realized her reaction was one of pure jealousy and not because they had a lot of work waiting for them.

"One would hope." Shelby's brows arched in amusement. "I think the girl's in love."

"Seriously?"

"Have you ever seen her act like she has this week?"

"You have a point." Mia worried her lip. Lindsey had always been more shy and not as invested in the college dating scene. Mia knew she was being selfish, but she hoped their friend's involvement with Rick didn't screw up their plans for the new business.

As if she'd read Mia's mind, Shelby sighed. "I can see it now. You two riding off into the sunset with your respective hunks, and me left to juggle Anything Goes."

Mia shook her head. "Lindsey maybe. It's not like that with David and me."

Shelby's gaze narrowed in an expectant frown. She waited as if there were supposed to be a punch line. "It's not like that with you and David?" She laughed. "You are so full of crap."

"I'm telling you, it was nothing. We were in Hawaii. No obligations, no hectic schedule. We had fun. I hope we'll still be friends." She shrugged. "I think we will."

Shelby's hazel eyes darkened with concern. "You almost sound like you believe that."

"I do. We're going to be very busy. I don't have time for him, and frankly, he won't have time for me." Mia made a show of getting comfortable, laying her head back and closing her eyes. "Think I'll grab a nap."

She knew Shelby was still staring, and she could keep staring until they landed in Dallas, for all Mia cared. She wasn't ready to have this conversation. She was too emotionally raw. Despite her brave words, she was a mess.

DAVID WAS SURPRISED to see his uncle Harrison's office door open at seven-thirty the next morning. After a brief knock, he entered as his uncle's head came up. Harrison set aside the contract he'd been perusing and stared at David over his reading glasses. "You look like hell."

"Red-eye, and I haven't been home yet." He wore the same clothes he had worn on the plane, khakis along with a yellow tennis shirt under a navy sports jacket. Totally inappropriate attire, but this was too important to delay.

Harrison anxiously glanced past him. "Is she here with you?"

"No. We had different flights." It was impossible, David knew, for someone to have visibly aged in the span of eight days, but his uncle's face looked drawn, his hair thinner and grayer, the combination packing a good five years on him. Most notable, however, was his cluttered desk. The man never tolerated anything out of place.

His dark eyes grew bleak. "She turned us down," Harrison said flatly.

David chose his words carefully. "She doesn't want to practice law anymore."

"What? How could she not want to practice law? She's brilliant. She's—Jesus. This doesn't make sense." He shook his head as if the act alone would turn the tide. "I thought she signed on with another firm."

"That had been my assumption, as well."

"So she doesn't have another job?" Harrison's frown lifted with hope.

"Not exactly. She's starting her own business." David checked his watch. He didn't have much time. "Look, I've been trying to get in touch with my father but he won't pick up his cell, and I've gotten the house's answering machine twice."

"He's with your mother," he said distractedly while staring out of his large plate glass window overlooking the Manhattan skyline. "Some charity golf thing in the Caymans."

"If I'd known about that, I'd forgotten." This time David reached for hope. "I'm surprised he'd leave. Something happen I should know about? Did we land another client?"

"No lifelines. You know he doesn't want to worry your mother, so he couldn't back out." His uncle leaned back in his chair and met David's eyes. "He had a lot of faith in you getting Butterfield back, figured you'd buy us some time."

Guilt cut deep. David had a lot of nerve wondering how his father could have left. Not when he himself had been gone a whole week, cavorting with Mia. "I know." David rubbed his stubbly jaw. He desperately needed a shave and a shower. "I want this prospective client's name and number."

His uncle's eyes narrowed. "Of course, but why?"

"I want to meet with him myself. If I can't convince him that we're the best firm for the job, then I'll take another run at Mia."

Harrison shook his head. "You're wasting your time. Your father and I have both met with his current attorney. The man's quite adamant."

David hadn't slept for one minute on the plane, and he was dead tired. Briefly he closed his eyes and scrubbed at his face. "I have to try," he said, not missing the curious gleam in Harrison's eye. "Anyway, what's the harm?"

"You have to ask?" His uncle pointedly looked past him through the open door. "Time isn't on our side, David."

He looked over his shoulder. It was still early, but quite a few employees already had arrived. Even so, the place was deathly quiet without the usual Monday morning chatter. In some of their hands were cups with the corner coffee kiosk logo. Up until last week, the firm had provided coffee, Danish and bagels each morning. Obviously the cutbacks had started.

"What have they been told?" David asked, taking a deep breath as he turned back to Harrison.

"Not much. For the record, I don't agree with that approach. Your father and Peter made that call."

David agreed with Harrison. Uncertainty was debilitating. But he continued to keep his opinion to himself. At the moment, he didn't feel he had the right to weigh in. Hell, he'd been off having fun with Mia instead of having to look into the employees' faces, tense from wondering who might be laid off first.

She'd been his confidante, his right arm for a week. He'd shared more with her than with any woman in his whole life. The pull to call her was strong, but he couldn't. Not yet. Not until he made this right.

MIA SPLASHED ice-cold water on her face, gazed blearily at the alarm clock she kept in her bathroom as a second line of defense and seriously thought about taking another shower just to wake up. It was crazy that she could be this exhausted after conking out the minute she got home from the airport the night before last, and then sleeping through half of yesterday. Apparently, she'd grossly underestimated the effects of jet lag.

Or her ability to shove David out of her mind.

"Aaargh." She squinted at her blurry reflection in the mirror. "Get a grip, Butterfield. He's only been back for one day." She dried her face and glanced again at the clock. Twenty-eight hours to be exact, so why hadn't he called already?

She muttered a curse and vigorously rubbed her eyes. This was exactly what she'd feared would happen. She was obsessing on when David would call, or if he would, or why he might not. It was insane, juvenile, completely useless, and yet her resolve melted after an hour. Of course she could always call him. No, absolutely not.

She'd given herself one day to recuperate before she had to dive into work. First, she had to purchase two new computers, go to the printers and proof the invoice and contract templates before the batches were run, and then pick up the keys to their new office and have new file cabinets installed. The place was small, configured in the shape of a shoe box, formerly leased by a dry cleaner who received and distributed laundry but did the work off premises. The cool thing was that while the front already had a counter and was large enough to accommodate a desk, a computer and the cabinets, the back led to an alley wide enough for pickups and deliveries for when they needed to transfer merchandise.

The warehouse she'd leased could've been in a more ideal location, but the price was right. While it would hold their initial inventory of bikes, power tools, sports equipment, party supplies and camping gear, there was still room to accommodate twice as much merchandise as they grew with demand.

She was excited to show Lindsey and Shelby everything. The office would be a big surprise since it was located only a block from the loft that she'd be sharing with them. Although there'd be some schlepping back and forth from the warehouse a couple times a week, more if they got really busy, she couldn't complain about the short commute.

Just thinking about Lindsey arriving tomorrow, and Shelby two days later, Mia got excited, and she decided she didn't need that second shower after all. She went to the closet and pulled out a pair of jeans and a sweater. Officially it was spring, but the March air was still chilly, which she very much resented after that balmy week in Hawaii.

Her cell phone rang. She froze for a second, trying to recall where she'd left it. The bathroom? No, the kitchen when she'd turned on the coffeepot. In her rush, she jammed her little toe on the corner of the dresser, and she limped the rest of the way.

She saw that it was Lindsey, and her heart thudded. "Hey, Linds." Mia glanced at the microwave clock. It was still early by Hawaii time. "You must be at the airport."

"Not exactly."

Mia frowned. She took another confirming look at the time. "Are you in Chicago already?"

"I'm still in Hawaii."

She leaned a hip against the counter and stifled a sigh. The hesitant tone told her Lindsey wouldn't be showing up tomorrow as planned. No sense in making her feel bad. "Bet you're having better weather than we are here."

"I'm sure," Lindsey said, with a nervous laugh, and then paused. "You're going to kill me."

Mia forgot about her injured toe, put too much weight on her foot and winced. "Promise I won't."

"Looks as if I won't be back for another two days. Is that going to totally screw up everyone?"

"Nope. I expect Shelby will be late, too. I think she underestimated the drive here."

"Then you'll be all alone. I can still get a flight—"

"Lindsey," Mia interrupted, drawing out her name in warning. "Don't you dare. I'm fine. Besides, we're our own bosses now."

Lindsey laughed. "I think we have to actually get the business off the ground first."

"And three or fours days are going to make a difference? I'm assuming you're still with Rick."

Lindsey sighed. "It's crazy, right?"

Mia smiled. "Go have fun. If you need more time, it's okay, too. I have everything covered."

"I'm sorry I didn't get to meet David. But I will when I get there."

Mia swallowed. "Yep. Now go."

After they hung up, Mia dropped her phone on the counter and stared at it as if it were the enemy. She could call him to make sure he'd arrived safely. Nothing wrong with showing concern for a friend. Right. Not a single thing transparent about that move. She exhaled with disgust, and picked up her phone. Who she really needed to call was Annabelle. Damn, she hoped she was back.

DAVID ARRIVED AT the restaurant eight minutes early. He'd never been here before and wasn't impressed with the drab decor. Heavy brown drapes, dark tan-colored walls adorned with too many autographed pictures of celebrities and tablecloths the shade of mud made the room dreary. Lit candles provided some relief, but not a single one sat straight in its holder.

Left up to him, he never would have brought a client, prospective or otherwise, to a place like this. He preferred Renae's; however, when he'd invited Mr. Peabody to dinner there yesterday, the man had flatly refused, referring to the popular Manhattan eatery as overpriced and pretentious.

This basement restaurant was Peabody's choice, a very interesting one considering the person he represented had to be filthy rich. The potential client still refused to be identified unless he decided to hire Pearson and Stern. Not entirely unusual, and in fact, such reticence often spoke to the affluence of the person, but David was frustrated and annoyed that he was forced to deal with a middle man, especially another attorney.

The blond hostess offered to seat David, but he declined, opting to wait for Peabody on an uncomfortable straight-back chair sitting against the wall near the hostess's stand.

He consulted his watch, mostly out of habit, and then checked his phone. No messages and no missed calls. And certainly no surprise. He'd been hypervigilant to the point of twice imagining his phone had rung when it hadn't. As much as he wasn't ready to talk to Mia, a part of him was disappointed that she hadn't called him, either. Hell, he hadn't been this foolish about a boy-girl phone game since middle school.

He glanced at the door, though not expecting Peabody for another five minutes. This was good timing, he thought, and pressed speed dial before he chickened out. He'd check in, explain he was at a dinner meeting and couldn't talk. She'd understand. After the fourth ring, he was sent to voice mail. In the middle of leaving a brief message, a seventy-something balding man with a thin face and a bulbous nose walked in. He wore a shabby brown suit that matched the drapes and carried a hat in his hand.

The smiling hostess greeted him by name. It was Peabody. A bit shocked, David disconnected the call and rose to introduce himself.

"Stan Peabody," the man confirmed with a firm handshake. "Heard good things about you, Pearson."

Good start that Peabody had heard of him. "Call me David."

"You call me Stan, of course."

"I have your usual table, Mr. Peabody," the hostess said, holding one red leather-bound menu against her chest, and then led the way to a corner spot oddly close to the kitchen.

It didn't surprise David when she laid the menu in front of him. Stan apparently didn't need one. "Scotch neat," she said to him, and then to David. "What can I get you to drink, sir?"

"I'll have the same."

Stan eyed him with amusement. "I drink the cheap stuff. You might want to be more specific."

David didn't know for certain, but he assumed he'd be measured by his response. "I'm not picky."

A faint smile tugged at the wrinkled corners of the older man's mouth. "You heard him, Sally."

"Be back in a jiff."

"I've got to say, David, when you called to invite me to dinner, I assumed you would've included Ms. Butterfield. I was looking forward to meeting her."

David silently cleared his throat, studied the man a moment. "I'm curious. Why specifically Mia Butterfield?"

"I have no idea." Peabody frowned. "Your father and I had this conversation last week."

"I apologize. I was away on vacation."

Stan Peabody might look like a rumpled old man, ready for his recliner and new flat screen to fill his time, but the shrewd gleam in his eye said he wasn't fooled. He knew damn well that David wouldn't be here without being fully informed.

"Look, Pearson, I don't have a team of lawyers working for me. It's me, one associate and my secretary, that's it. Both of them have been ready to retire for five years, and so have I." He paused while the hostess set down their drinks and informed them their waitress would be with them right away.

Stan took an unhurried sip of his scotch before continuing. "This is the last client I have on my books. I gave my word I would continue to administer the estate until a suitable replacement could be found. This client has been with me for thirty-three years. I take that kind of loyalty seriously," he said, settling back in his chair and looking infinitely tired.

"I understand," David said, hope surging. The man was motivated and needed a slight push. "We at Pearson and Stern also value that kind of loyalty. That's why I wanted to meet you in person and assure you that this account is important to us, and would have my undivided attention. I know my father explained that Ms. Butterfield isn't an estate attorney, but what we would bill for my time would be in accordance with what she, as a junior associate, would bill."

Peabody's eyebrows drew together in alarmed concern. "Are you saying Ms. Butterfield isn't available?"

David seriously wanted to plead the Fifth. Admitting Mia was no longer with the firm would likely end negotiations. "Not at the present time."

Peabody slowly shook his head. "I don't think you do understand. My client wants Ms. Butterfield in charge, period. If that's not an option, then we'll go elsewhere."

David's insides clenched. "Would you at least tell me why?"

"Couldn't say." He gave a weary shrug. "Now that business is over," he said, signaling the waiter, "may I suggest the porterhouse steak and sautéed mushrooms?"

David's stomach churned.

13

BY THE END OF her third day back in New York, Mia returned to her loft, feeling more overwhelmed than she'd ever dreamed. It wasn't just that Shelby and Lindsey had both been delayed, or that Annabelle wasn't around, or even that Mia had spent the day hustling all over Midtown tying up loose ends and discovering how many more frivolous details had fallen through the cracks. A big part of her problem was that she was distracted and annoyed for making stupid errors that were costing her time and energy. She was usually so organized.

She refused to think this was a result of the disjointed voice mail David had left yesterday evening. She'd just hit the shower when he called, and because he mentioned he was at a dinner meeting she couldn't call him back. What had gotten to her though, was the remoteness in his voice. But she'd heard the background noise so she knew he'd made the call in public, which could account for his curtness. As a lawyer she knew better than to make premature assumptions.

Except she wasn't a lawyer anymore. Only according to the New York Bar Association, of which she was still a member. The thought kind of depressed her, although it made no sense. She should have felt liberated, anxious to put all the planning and strategizing of Anything Goes into action, and she was eager. She was. But it was weird not having an office full of people to go to, where a stack of pink message slips collected on the corner of her desk. It was even weirder to not see David every day.

She dropped her purse and keys on the metal-and-wood console table where she stacked her mail, and then checked the thermostat. Grudgingly she turned up the heat. It was officially spring, but obviously someone hadn't gotten the memo. She had a bad feeling it would be another couple of weeks before she could store her sweaters.

After briefly considering slapping a tuna sandwich together for dinner, she decided it was too late to eat, and she wasn't hungry enough anyway. She crawled onto her bed and lay on top of the old worn patchwork quilt her grandmother had made for Mia's fifth birthday. She'd already broken down once and returned David's call, but that had been midafternoon and she decided against leaving a message. Poor guy had to be in a ton of meetings after being away for so long.

Her cell rang, and in her current state of mind, she was convinced it was either Shelby or Lindsey, calling about yet another delay. But when she rolled over and grabbed the phone off the nightstand, her pulse leaped when she saw that it was David.

"Hello?"

"Mia, I'm glad I caught you."

"I just got home, and I can finally breathe again."

"I know what you mean. I've been in meetings all day."

"I figured. Are you still at the office?"

"Oh, yeah." He paused, the silence lasting too long, long enough for a slew of bad scenarios to flit through her head, and her heart started to sink. "I miss you."

She smiled, briefly closed her eyes. "I miss you, too," she said softly, feeling the tension melt from her cramped neck and shoulders.

"I know it's late, but any chance you'd like to grab some dinner?"

"Sure." Her gaze darted to the clock, and then at her old jeans and bulky sweater. "When and where?"

"Now? Renae's?"

Renae's? She'd only been there once, with David, in fact, and another attorney from Pearson and Stern, but only because they'd taken a client there to be wined and dined. She'd thought then that the setting would have been romantic if the dinner hadn't been about business. Although she was touched that David had chosen such a fine restaurant, it wouldn't do tonight. "How about someplace more casual and give me forty minutes?"

"You got it. Name the place."

"Feel like pizza?"

David hesitated. "From Renae's to a pizza joint."

"You asked." She carried the phone with her to the closet and sifted through her clothes, looking for a pair of decent slacks.

"Mea culpa. You have a place in mind? A *quiet* place?"

Grinning, she gave him a name and address, hung up and then charged into the bathroom. She needed a quick shower and her makeup refreshed. She wanted to look nice for him, which was ridiculous on so many levels. Not only had he already seen her at her worse, but she was also not supposed to be this excited that he'd called. At this point in her life, it was supposed to be all about the work ahead. She didn't care. For tonight, she was damn happy.

DAVID ARRIVED AT the quaint neighborhood restaurant first, hoping for a secluded table. The place Mia chose was nicer than he expected, quiet and small with about a dozen tables and booths, only half of which were occupied. No hostess was in sight, so he grabbed a table that was far enough away from the kitchen and other diners where he and Mia could have a private conversation.

He sat facing the door, and loosened his tie. The damn thing felt as if it were going to choke him to death. Not wearing one while he was in Hawaii had felt odd at first, though he'd gotten used to the freedom quickly. But it wasn't about the tie. His nerves were shot. Even the infamous bar exam that put the fear of God into the most arrogant law student had been a breeze compared to his mission tonight.

The waitress showed up, and tempted to throw back a double scotch, he ordered a beer he likely wouldn't touch. He hoped like hell it wasn't a mistake to bring Mia to a restaurant to make the offer. He'd reasoned that it was as close to keeping the tone as businesslike as possible. Asking her to the office would have been awkward.

Inviting her to his apartment was out, as was going to hers. This conversation, one he'd sworn last week he'd never have with her, was going to be tough enough, and he needed to stay focused. If she showed the slightest distress, or even hinted that she thought what had happened between them in Hawaii had been a lie, he didn't trust himself not to pull her into his arms, tell her how much he loved her and damn everything else.

At least sticking to a public forum gave him a fighting chance to do right by his family and the employees who counted on the firm. Reputations, livelihoods, honor— so much more than his happiness was at stake. Either way though, guilt held him hostage. She hadn't said the words, but he was pretty sure she loved him, too. The possibility was the only thing that gave him comfort and courage. But at the same time, it was her feelings for him that gave him the power to hurt her. And if he did, he'd never forgive himself.

The bell over the restaurant's door signaled the arrival of a newcomer. But he'd been watching intently and already knew it was Mia. Something inside of him went soft as he watched her cross the threshold. Her hair was down, dark and shiny and skimming the shoulders of her red sweater. She spotted him the second he started to rise, and her lips curved into a smile that lit up her beautiful green eyes. He saw love there, whether she knew it yet or not. But did she love him enough to trust him?

Mia was glad to see that there weren't many people in the restaurant. Still, she wished she'd thought quickly enough to invite him over to her loft instead. The best she could've done was tuna or grilled cheese sandwiches and the place was a bit messy, but she doubted he would've cared.

He came around the table, smiled and pulled out the chair across from the one he'd been using. "Hi."

Something was wrong. His smile seemed strained. And why didn't he want her sitting in the chair beside him? When he gave her a light, brotherly peck on the cheek, she knew she wasn't imagining things.

"Hi back," she said, trying to keep her tone breezy, even though her brain immediately went to that bad place.

She calmly sat down and stowed her purse on the vacant seat where her butt should've been. Friends, right? From the very beginning, all she wanted was a causal relationship once they'd returned, she reminded herself.

"What would you like to drink?" he asked as he reclaimed his chair.

"I think I'll stick with water." She eyed his untouched mug of beer, his loosened tie. "I have another busy day tomorrow."

"How are things going?" he asked, looking oddly serious. This was his office demeanor, from the staid expression to the polite tone of his voice. He sounded nothing like the man who called her less than an hour ago. The one who'd told her he missed her.

Disappointment rose in her throat, but she stayed cool. "It's hectic. But the cavalry arrives tomorrow, so that'll help."

His eyebrows dipped in a puzzled frown.

"Shelby and Lindsey," she reminded him.

"Ah. Aren't they supposed to be here already?"

"Shelby is driving from Houston and got slowed down by construction. Lindsey apparently is having one hell of a good time with her new guy."

"Not fair to you."

"It's not fair that they have to move all their stuff." She shrugged. "Everything works out in the long run.

What about you? Did you get dumped with a ton of motions and briefs?"

"Let's just say I don't see a vacation in my near future," he said with a wry smile, and for a moment he seemed to relax.

"I know what you mean." She got over her anxiousness long enough to notice that under his tan, he looked really tired, more than usual, as if he hadn't been sleeping well. True, they'd had a few marathon nights in Hawaii when neither of them had slept much, but there had been long, lazy afternoon naps and time spent lounging by the pool.

God, she missed those days. The memories alone made her flush with warm pleasure, and she looked into his dark eyes, willing him to remember them, too.

He smiled. "So, tell me what specifically has been keeping you so busy."

She took a long, slow sip of the water that had already been placed on the table. "A lot of running around, receiving office furniture and supplies, lining up inventory. Oh, and trying to get six crummy cabinets installed. You'd think that would be easy, right?"

"If you can get tradesmen to show up on time, I call that progress."

"See, that's the problem...they're supposed to actually show up. Silly me."

His mouth curved in a reasonable facsimile of a smile, but it wasn't right. She knew that his real smile was ever so slightly lopsided, hiking up a bit more on the right and deepening the groove in his cheek. His real smile always reached his eyes and made her gooey inside. This one put her on edge.

"What about you? Anything interesting happening at

the office?" she asked, wondering if a case had soured, which would account for his tension.

He started to shake his head, and then with a wry expression said, "Sam Glasser got cited for contempt for shooting off his mouth, and took a night in jail rather than cough up the ten grand."

"Judge Palmer, right?"

"Who else?"

Mia bit off a laugh. "But Sam? The guy is always so stoic. Palmer had to have really pissed him off."

"Palmer pisses everyone off."

"True." Mia remembered the first time she stood in front of the grouchy old judge. He looked like someone's doting grandfather but had the bite of an angry pit bull. "He's got to be close to retirement age."

"The guy needs a hobby. He's never in a hurry to get out of court. If it's a nice day, you know Lancaster and Silva will be anxious to get on the golf course."

Mia laughed, feeling more relaxed. "I'd been at the firm about a month when someone warned me about Palmer. I was so nervous the morning I was going before him, and I walked in, saw this guy who looked like Santa Claus and figured I'd been punked."

"He looks deceptive, all right, and he loves breaking in baby attorneys."

Mia snorted. "Yeah, and you said he doesn't have a hobby."

At that, David chuckled. For a second, she thought he was going to reach for her hand, but he wrapped his fingers around his mug instead.

"Yep, Palmer had a good old time with me. Fifteen minutes in, and I seriously wanted to take his head off. I just knew I'd end up fined for contempt, and you would give me my walking papers."

"Never would've happened." He looked as if he were about to say something else, but stopped and inhaled deeply. "It seems like a long time ago."

"It does." Mia felt the mood shift again and, desperate to hang on, she asked, "Hey, did Libby finally figure out how to work the new cappuccino machine?"

David frowned. He clearly had no idea what she was talking about, and of course he wouldn't. That sort of office minutia escaped his notice.

The waitress appeared and described the two specials of the night. While David listened, Mia studied him. His posture was too rigid, his features tight and a telling tic in his jaw betrayed the tension he was trying to hide. If she were to quiz him on the waitress's spiel, Mia doubted he'd have heard a word.

"Thank you," he politely told the woman. "If you wouldn't mind giving us another minute."

"No problem." The young brunette smiled apologetically. "Just to let you know, we do close in an hour."

"Thank you," he said again, and after she left, glanced at his watch and winced. "Nine-thirty already."

"I hope you don't have to go back to the office."

He gave a noncommittal shrug of one shoulder.

"Oh, David." To her shame, it finally struck her that his considerable workload had been made worse by her resignation. How hadn't she gotten that sooner? "Have you found a replacement for me yet?"

He met her eyes and slowly shook his head.

"Any candidates?"

"One."

"Good." She was glad because she hated that he had

to take up the slack. But a tiny part of her disliked the idea of being replaced. Knowing it would be someone else working alongside David. She hoped it was a guy. "How far along are you in the interview process?"

He picked up his beer and took a small sip, his gaze still level with hers. "We want you back, Mia."

She blinked, reared her head. "What?"

"Naturally, there's a promotion and raise involved."

She studied him, her heart hammering her breastbone. "Is this a joke?"

"No." He tugged at his already loosened tie. "I'm making you an official offer."

"This is insane. I have the new business to—I told you I didn't want to practice law anymore." She shook her head, saddened that he could sit there and show no emotion.

"I understand." He glanced away. "I thought perhaps a promotion and raise might give you new perspective."

She stared blankly at him, the memory of last week fading like an old, mistreated photograph. Had he listened to her at all? "Whose idea was this?"

He hesitated. "My father's. Harrison and Peter also are in agreement. We're all in agreement," he corrected.

"I don't understand." She shook her head again, overwhelmed with confusion, thoughts swirling and crashing in her head. "Why?"

"You're a brilliant attorney. We simply want you back."

The old David sat before her, professional, stoic, too rigid, as if one tiny slip would expose him, that he'd give her a glimpse of the man who'd made passionate love to her and picked macadamia nuts out of his ice cream.

"I've barely spoken to your father or your uncle in the three years I worked there."

"Trust me, they keep abreast of everything that goes on at Pearson and Stern, including associates' performances."

"I can understand offering a raise to get someone back, but a promotion? Karen, Ron and Steve have all been there longer than me. What would they say about this?"

"May I assume from your concern that you're considering our offer?" He sat there, waiting, his dark unfathomable eyes giving nothing away.

She stared back, clenching her teeth, her anger growing. "You know what, David, screw you. Or sorry, maybe I should call you 'Mr. Pearson'."

Regret flickered in his face. "Mia." He started to reach for her hand again, but clearly saw he wasn't welcome and stopped himself.

She folded her hands in her lap under the table. A horrible, devastating thought suddenly occurred to her. Fear tripped her up and she didn't know if she had the guts to ask the question. No, she couldn't ignore it. "Did you know about the offer before Hawaii?"

Not so much as an eyelash moved. "Yes."

For a second she thought she was going to be sick. Even if she wanted to hurl an accusation at him, she couldn't speak.

"My going to Hawaii had nothing to do with the firm. That was strictly personal." His composure faltered. A hint of desperation echoed in the deep resonance of his voice. "I wanted to be with you, Mia. Please believe that."

She wanted to believe him, and a part of her did. She

was a good judge of character, and she'd known him a long time. David was an honorable man. Still, he'd given up so much of himself for the firm. It wouldn't be a leap to give them up, as well. "You knew you'd eventually be making the offer, and if I were to accept, where would that leave us?"

"I admit, that's tricky. More for the sake of office morale than anything, we'd have to keep our relationship private."

"Who knew you went to Hawaii?"

"My father and Harrison."

"Did *they* know it was personal?" she asked, feeling as if she were being torn in half, and resenting his ability to keep his reactions under such tight control.

"I didn't spell it out, no."

So they likely thought the sweet-talking to lure her back was all part of the job, and for all she knew, it had been. The pain of that thought cut so deep it hurt just to breathe.

"Off the record, I didn't want to make this offer, but I virtually had no choice."

"Really?" She scoffed. He'd had a choice. They both knew that.

Yet the agony in his face looked real. "What I'm about to tell you is strictly confidential. We've had some setbacks at the firm. For reasons that have nothing to do with our performance, two of our largest clients are jumping ship."

"Who?" she asked, stunned.

"I'd rather not go into details. There's been no official announcement yet."

After all they'd shared in Hawaii, his secrecy hurt.

"Then how can you afford to offer me a raise and a promotion?"

"A potential new client has asked for you to manage their estate, which includes a very large charitable foundation."

"What? Who? I don't do estate planning."

"They won't identify themselves unless we meet their terms. Unfortunately, you're a deal-breaker."

She shook her head, still confused over who would make such a demand. "I have my own commitments—"

"What about coming in part-time?"

Mia's brain could barely handle the stream of information. But one thing registered clearly. The firm was desperate, so was David. And sadly, desperate men did desperate things.

14

"I DON'T REMEMBER THIS PLACE being so small," Shelby said, trailing Mia through the loft. "Good thing all my stuff is going straight to storage."

"Our names are on a list for a three-bedroom, but it's going to be a while." Mia sidestepped Lindsey's enormous suitcase and led Shelby into the tiny second bedroom, or so named by the landlord. Mia had seen bigger walk-in closets.

"It's not as if we'll be at home much." Shelby shrugged. "When did Lindsey get here?"

"About twenty minutes ago. She went to get us coffee."

Shelby studied the small room. "How are we divvying up space?"

"I figured we'd discuss it when Lindsey got back."

"She talk to you about Rick?"

Mia shook her head. "Like I said, she hasn't been here long."

"She's still being really secretive. I think she may be putting up a front. She say anything at all to you?"

They heard the front door open and then Lindsey call out, "It's just me. I have coffee and lattes."

"Caffeine. Good." Mia massaged her left temple as they went to meet Lindsey in the kitchen. She really didn't want to talk about their friend's love problems because that meant the conversation would inevitably turn to David, and Mia so wasn't ready for that to happen. Not that she had much choice. She had a decision to make, and it involved her friends.

Lindsey's blond hair was tied back in a haphazard ponytail, the darkness under her eyes making her look as bad as Mia felt. "Did you just get here?" Lindsey asked Shelby.

"Yep. Traffic was brutal."

"You're going to be so sorry you brought that cute little Mustang convertible of yours."

"That's right," Shelby said. "Rub it in."

Lindsey grinned, looking as if she hadn't a care in the world. So maybe everything was good with Rick. Somehow that didn't make Mia feel better, and being a bitch by not sharing in her friend's happiness made her feel even worse.

The throbbing at Mia's temple grew worse. She grabbed a coffee Lindsey had set on the counter. "Guys, I know you just got here, but there's something I have to discuss with you."

"Uh-oh." Shelby scooped up a latte. "I don't like that tone."

Mia led the way into the living room, then took the chrome director's chair and left the tan leather couch for them.

She was exhausted from staying up most of the night, weighing the pros and cons of returning to the firm, even if it was only part-time. The identity of the potential client still puzzled her. Who could possibly want her so badly that they were holding the firm hostage? She didn't know anybody with that kind of money. Not personally anyway. Unless they were already a client that she'd met at some point.

Of all the reasons not to return to the firm, the emotional toll of seeing David weighed the most heavily. She desperately wanted to believe he wasn't the kind of man who would have used her to meet his objective, but she'd be a fool to ignore how much his family and the firm's reputation meant to him.

And of course, there was the launch of Anything Goes to consider...

God, she hated even bringing up the subject. They had so much work to do before next Monday when their first ad would hit the papers and the flyers were to be distributed telling all of New York City they'd be open for business. No one, least of all her, needed to be distracted by David or his problem.

She waited until they were both curled up on opposite corners of the couch. "David wants me to go back to the firm."

"You're kidding." Shelby's eyes narrowed. "He knows about Anything Goes, right?"

Lindsey looked confused. "But if you're working for him again, then how can you see each other?"

"I'm not worried about that," Mia said, annoyed that her voice cracked.

"Meaning?" Shelby asked.

"Could we stay on point?"

Not the slightest bit deterred by her no-nonsense tone, they both said, "No."

Mia sighed, then gave them an abbreviated and less personal version of their meeting last night, careful not to give away too much about the firm's trouble or her misery. Oddly she still felt protective toward David and Pearson and Stern in general. Of course, as an employer, they had been good to her and there was no reason not to preserve their privacy.

After a long, thoughtful silence, it was Shelby who asked, "So what are you going to do?"

"I don't know. That's what we need to discuss."

Lindsey frowned. "Didn't you say he's in kind of a jam?"

"Yes, but that doesn't mean it has to be my problem." Mia bit her lower lip. She hadn't meant to sound sharp.

"Okay," Shelby drawled. "What are you not telling us?"

Damn, as good as David was at concealing his feelings, Mia was terrible at it. The stupid bastard. He even had that over her. She sipped her coffee, groping wildly for some witty, distracting remark. The only thing that emerged was a startling awareness of how much her resentment toward David had been building. "Guess I know why he followed me to Hawaii."

Shelby's eyes widened, and she seemed truly stunned. "You don't think that whole thing was a ploy to get you back."

She sighed. "What am I supposed to think?"

"I saw him with you, Mia. There is no way that man was there for any reason other than he's in love with you."

At the outrageous claim, Mia snorted, and then to

her utter horror, hope actually filled her chest. "Right. You couldn't be further off base."

"Come on, girl, you're not that stupid."

"Shelby," Lindsey admonished in a low hushed voice.

"You didn't see them together like I did," Shelby said testily. "It's crazy to think that he doesn't—Okay, look, shoving all that 'he loves me, he loves me not' crap aside, let's talk about this rationally."

The menacing look that Lindsey gave Shelby almost made Mia smile. Usually it was her and Shelby who went head to head, and Lindsey who smoothed things over.

"From what I understand," Shelby continued, unfazed, "you can go back part-time, yes?"

Mia nodded absently, her thoughts lagging. Shelby didn't know what she was talking about. Oh, for a few moments last week, Mia had foolishly thought her and David's physical attraction to each other had crossed a threshold, but now she knew better. She alone had made the leap to love. That's what had her so upset. It wasn't lust or infatuation or the thrill of finally getting something that had been withheld from her. She'd fallen in love with him. But how could she?

"Mia, are you listening?"

"Yes," she lied, and realized she'd missed a lot. Somehow, in those few moments of inattention, Shelby had swung Lindsey to her side. They both looked at her with a mixture of concern and expectation.

"If you didn't mind working a couple of days a week," Shelby said, "it would be kind of nice to have money for rent and such without dipping into savings or into the business fund."

"But only if you want to," Lindsey said, and Shelby gave her the eye.

Mia sighed. "Like I don't know you two are trying to manipulate me."

"Is it working?" Shelby asked, and then offered a faint smile. "I know you, sweetie, you're going to throw yourself into work and never give yourself the chance to find out if what you have with David is real."

"I don't see how going back to the firm will help me do that," Mia muttered crossly. "Anyway, I don't want to be a practicing lawyer."

"Hmm, I hadn't considered that," Lindsey said thoughtfully, her head cocked to the side as she stared speculatively at Mia. "But have you considered that it wasn't practicing law you were running away from?"

IT WAS AFTER FIVE when David's private line rang, and he inhaled a deep calming breath before picking up the receiver. He knew it was her. "Mia?"

She hesitated. "Yes."

"Did Shelby and Lindsey make it in all right?" About an hour ago, he'd been ready to go knock down her door. He was tired from lack of sleep and stressed to the max from the gloomy tension hanging over the office, to which he'd contributed with his foul mood. Everyone, including his good-natured assistant, had steered clear of him all day. Suited him just fine.

She softly cleared her throat. "Yes, they did."

"Good." This time he paused, tempted to tell her that he didn't want to know her answer, to forget about the job. What he really wanted was to ask if she'd catch the next flight back to Hawaii with him. "So you've thought about the offer?"

"I discussed it with Shelby and Lindsey, considering they are my business partners and will be impacted by my decision." She sounded stiff, formal. What had he expected? "I have—"

"Can we do this in person?"

"I don't see the point."

He rubbed the knot at the back of his neck. "We didn't finish our dinner last night."

After a long silence, she said, "I still don't see the point."

"Mia, please. I'm not the enemy."

"I never said you were. This is business. That's all. And frankly, I'm surprised you're not more eager to hear my answer." She paused. "This being such an urgent matter."

He squeezed his tired eyes shut, but only for a second, and then stared at his jacket hanging limply on the back of his door. He'd hoped she would have mellowed out over night, remember the things they'd said to each other in Hawaii, but she sounded angrier today. "I want to see you."

"David, please, don't make this harder than it already is."

Damn her. She should have trusted him. Obviously she didn't. "Fine. What's your answer?" His voice was all business. It seemed that's what she wanted.

"I have my own terms. I work two days a week until I familiarize myself with the client and the type of trusts that need to be established. Those two days will be at my discretion, and later, after the groundwork is complete, I come in only one day a week."

"All right," he said slowly, irritation with himself

deepening because he was already thinking ahead to what that meant for them personally.

"I'm not finished," she said, her tone equally curt.

"Go on." Probably better that they hadn't meant in person. This was intolerable.

"I won't take the promotion, but I will take the raise. And I want Karen Flint working with me. She's a good attorney and can easily replace me when the time comes that I can permanently separate myself from the firm."

Something about the way her voice lowered at the end, how she clearly enunciated each word, fed David's uneasiness. Now *this* was personal. It was him she wanted out of her life, not the firm. He went numb. "Anything else?"

"No, I—" She softly cleared her throat. He might have interpreted the pause as regret, but chose not to. "I think that's it."

"Fine. Pearson and Stern agrees to your terms. We'll draw up a contract. In the meantime, I'll need to call our new client and set up an appointment. What day can you come in?"

"I'll call and let you know."

"Great. I'll talk to you then." He started to pull the receiver away from his ear, and stopped. "Thank you," he said, his words cut short by the disconnecting click.

AS SOON AS MIA GOT INTO the elevator, she tugged at the hem of her suit jacket, then at the cuffs, and finally brushed some lint off her skirt. It was ridiculous to be so nervous. She didn't recall her first day at the firm being this bad, although in all likelihood it had been worse. Then again, she hadn't yet slept with her boss.

She groaned, smoothed back the hair that she'd rolled into a French twist, glad she'd decided to come in extra early. David would be there, but no one else yet. Any awkward moments between them would be over and done with before the others arrived.

Part of her phone conversation with David popped unbidden into her head. She'd had too many unguarded moments like that since she'd last spoken to him. Admittedly she'd been one shade short of abrupt, and she shouldn't have expected him to grovel or beg her forgiveness or make some grand, outrageous gesture like show up at her door with three dozen roses.

But a small part of her had longed for him to ignore the crap she'd dished out, ride in on a stupid horse and use his mouth, hands and body to show her how wrong she was. Whisper sweet nothings until she was convinced. She wanted her big, strong hero back. She honestly hadn't expected him to throw her coldness back at her.

The elevator dinged its arrival. God, she hoped this wasn't a mistake. Once she spoke with the new client and became immersed in work, it would be okay, she assured herself as the doors slid open.

For a split second she thought she'd pressed the wrong button. There were people, a good many of them, sitting in their cubicles or at their desks or hovering over someone else's. One by one they looked up, varying degrees of surprise registering on their faces as they watched her leave the elevator.

She knew all of the junior associates, of course, and most of the admin staff, but no one looked particularly happy to see her. Not that she expected a welcoming committee, but wow, what a way to come back. What the hell had David told them about her return?

"Good morning," she said to Laura, the receptionist, who gave her the first genuine smile.

"Hi, Mia, you're looking nice and tan—lucky you," she said, her smile turning enigmatic. "Bet you're here for your plant."

"My plant?"

Laura gestured toward the bushy green fern sitting at the end of the reception counter.

Mia recognized it now. A client had sent it to her as a thank-you last year. "To tell you the truth, I'd forgotten about it. Looks good there, though…" Her voice trailed off when it struck her that there were no fresh flowers.

No gigantic seasonal arrangement where the plant now sat, and nothing equally decadent and exotic sitting on a table in the foyer. She glanced over her shoulder. The waiting area was also bare. A few tall palms and ficus helped liven up the place, but it was obvious that just as many had been removed. And this was the main floor. No telling what the two lower floors looked like.

"Mia?"

At the sound of David's voice, she turned her head and saw him standing in the hall leading to his office, gesturing for her to follow.

"The plant looks good, Laura, better than when I had it. Keep it," she said, before heading toward David, her mind scrambling to make sense of the changes that had taken place in only three weeks and ignoring the way her heart had been crushed just by looking at him.

"You're early," he said with a scant curve of his mouth.

"So is everyone else. What's going on?"

"Let's wait until we get to the conference room," he said in a hushed voice. "You might grab some coffee on the way. There's no service set up there yet."

They got to the employee break room, and David waited outside while she got her coffee. She noticed the absence of both cappuccino machines and the hot chocolate dispenser. There was milk, none of the fancy flavored creams. No trays of donuts and bagels or fresh fruit, which in the past had been provided for the employees. Maybe because it was too early yet. She didn't think so. The firm's problems clearly were bigger and more serious than she thought.

Thank God there was still coffee, and she quickly poured a cup, eager to get out of the dismal room. That the perks had been so quickly withdrawn told her more than David had been willing to confide. The cutbacks had to really depress him. The firm had always been prosperous. This had to be hard for David's whole family to accept.

He eyed her cup of black coffee. "I've ordered some fruit, Danish and juice to be brought to the conference room twenty minutes before the client arrives," he said, his tone bordering on apologetic. "You can get something to eat then."

"I'm fine. What time is the meeting?" They'd started down the hall again, their shoulders occasionally brushing, and she vividly remembered the times when the slightest innocent touch would rattle her concentration. Now, after Hawaii, after the other night and his impersonal offer to return, she honestly didn't know what she should feel.

"Not until nine." He stopped in front of her old office, small and empty but for the desk and file cabinet. "I didn't even ask, is using your old office okay with you?"

"Of course." She tried not to feel insulted. She had taken the raise after all. Now she wasn't sure she wanted it. "Is there a specific reason we're going to the conference room now?"

"We need to talk before our meeting." He studied her face with those serious brown eyes of his, just like he had the moment before he'd kissed her for the first time. The flash of memory undercut her resolve, and her foolish heart twisted with longing. "I figured you might be more comfortable there."

She understood now. The conference room was mostly glass; his office was more private. "It doesn't matter where we are, David. I think we both know we're safe." If she'd meant to wound him, his flinch told her she'd gotten close to the mark with her sarcasm.

Then his features tightened. "All right, my office then."

She should have found satisfaction in eliciting a reaction, but all she felt was sad as she followed him. Her sense of vulnerability had prompted the needless barb. Too late to do anything about it but accept his retreat behind the mask.

He closed the door while she sat in one of the chairs facing his desk. "I had a contract drawn up guaranteeing your salary on a daily basis," he said, as he took his seat, his hand protecting his red tie as he leaned forward to open the bottom drawer. "Without obligation on your part."

"How bad is it?"

His questioning eyes met hers. "I'm not sure I follow."

"With the firm. Will there be layoffs?"

He leaned back, shoving a hand through his hair. "Obviously we're trying to avoid that."

"But everyone's worried."

His humorless lips lifted slightly, his gaze drifting toward the door. "You see how early they're all showing up. They see the cutbacks. They're wondering what's next."

"They should be told the truth." She didn't care that it wasn't her business, although to some degree she could justify her concern. "Uncertainty is far more harmful to morale."

"I couldn't agree more," he said, giving her an odd look. He took his time studying her face. "But it's not my call."

She wasn't talking about them, if that's what he thought. And even if she was, at least he'd gotten it right. "I wish you could get through to him," she said, then added, "your father."

"He's doing everything he knows how to do." David sighed, touched a finger to his lips like he did when he was trying to think something through. "Between us? Neither he nor Harrison is drawing a salary. They aren't being cavalier about the problem."

"And you?"

He drew back slightly. The question clearly had startled him. He said nothing for a long, drawn-out moment. "No."

Mia's temple started throbbing again. Damn it. "Give me the contract."

At her abruptness, his mouth tightened with irritation, but he did as she asked.

"I'm not accepting the raise," she said, and tore the contract in half.

15

THE SECOND DAY at the office Mia sat at her old desk, staring at a stack of contracts, sorely tempted to tell David the deal was off. First, she didn't like the new client. Oh, Stan Peabody was nice enough, but he should never have been overseeing this massive an undertaking, and with only an associate and a paralegal to assist him. Poor guy, he simply wanted the reins passed so he could retire. What had Mia irked was that the person he represented still hadn't revealed his identity. Pompous ass.

But that was the least of Mia's complaints. The atmosphere around the office was barely tolerable. The senior Mr. Pearson was still refusing to clue in the employees as to what was happening. With no good reason not to, everyone feared for their jobs and wondered whose job Mia had stolen by returning. She was unarguably persona non grata.

The icing on the cake? The employees didn't know the half of it yet. Unknowingly they had every reason to question why she'd been put in charge of this particular account. This wasn't her forte. She wasn't a tax attorney or an estate-planning attorney. There were a dozen other lawyers at the firm who were eminently more quali-fied to head the team, and yes, the account was colos-sal enough to require a team. Assets had been poorly managed, and the revenue pools shamefully shallow. The foundation should've been making money hand-over-fist. Pearson and Stern had more work to do than had been anticipated. The account would make them *beaucoup* bucks, and that made it even more difficult for Mia to extricate herself from her agreement.

Her prominent role also meant that once word was out about her project, Mia was about to go from persona non grata to pariah in the staff's estimation, with the exception of Karen Flint, but that was only because the woman had to work with her so if Karen did harbor any resentment, she kept a close lid on it.

The worst thing, by far, was David himself. Not that he'd done anything egregious, but working close to him was killing her. She seriously doubted if she would've agreed to return had she known he would directly over-see the account. She'd made the mistake of assuming she was in charge, but to be fair, it was Peabody who'd announced at the end of the meeting that David's in-volvement was also required. That he'd seemed equally surprised was the reason she hadn't walked out that very minute.

Well, not the only reason. Damned if she hadn't soft-ened toward David when the first retainer check had exchanged hands, and the king of stone faces had been unable to hide a flash of relief. Nothing major sure. A flicker in his eyes, a small twitch at the right side of his mouth, a slight bob of his Adam's apple. No one but her would have noticed. The knowledge both warmed her and made her want to throw her stapler at the wall.

"Knock, knock."

She looked up to find Karen standing in her doorway holding two mugs. "Come in."

"Am I interrupting? I can come back."

"No, please." Mia motioned to the plain straight-back guest chair someone had scraped up for her.

"I brought coffee, if you're interested."

"Very." She reached for the mug Karen set on the desk. "Thanks. I'm sure this is lunch."

Karen sat down. "I have some instant soup packets in my desk if you'd like." Then she added dourly, "I believe we still have hot water in the break room."

Mia glanced at her over the rim of her cup, but said nothing and sipped.

Karen flushed. "Sorry, I shouldn't have said that."

"No worries. Hard to miss the tension around here."

"Yeah, that's for sure. Look, I know that you asked me to help with this account, and I just wanted to say I'm grateful."

Mia needed to tread carefully. "Who told you that?"

The older woman's dark brows furrowed as if she didn't understand why Mia wouldn't know such an obvious answer. "David."

"Ah." That didn't make her happy. He needed to communicate better. As far as Mia knew, *everything* was hush-hush.

"He warned me not to tell anyone or discuss the account with the others, but clearly that excludes you." She shrugged. "I had to thank you. My husband lost his job two months ago, and we depend on my salary. Being involved with this account provides some job security. At least I'm hoping." She worried her lower lip. "It's just so scary around here now. The not knowing is wearing thin on everyone."

"I understand," Mia said in a slow and cautious voice.

"I'm not pumping you for information," Karen said quickly. "Please don't think that."

"Why should I? I don't know anything."

Karen looked at her with a doubtful expression. "I just figured since you and David—" She seemed really nervous now. "You know, I should go." Abruptly she stood.

Uneasiness crawled up Mia's spine. Of course she'd heard whispers, saw the accusing looks, but she didn't totally understand what chatter was being disseminated. "Karen, wait." While Mia got up and closed the office door, she motioned the woman to reclaim her seat. Maybe it was wiser to let the matter drop, but she liked and trusted Karen, who'd never been one to gossip, and if Mia were ever going to find out what was being muttered in the office bullpen, this seemed like her chance.

Mia sat down again and faced Karen, who looked as if she'd rather be stuck in an airless cab during a rush hour jam.

She cleared her throat, wondering how to begin diplomatically. "I owe you a thanks as well for not treating me like I have leprosy," she said, and Karen blanched, nervously tucking her curly auburn hair behind her ear. "I'm fully aware most of the associates are unhappy that I've returned to the firm," Mia continued. "I don't blame them, and it won't help when they find out more about this mystery account. I can assure you that I'm not here at anyone's expense. I can't be more specific, and I doubt trying to reassure the rest of them would do any good because they probably wouldn't believe me."

"No," Karen agreed softly, surprising Mia with her easy candor. "They wouldn't. Frankly, I'd leave it alone, Mia."

She wished she could, but it was eating at her, undermining her concentration. "It's needless tension. What puzzles me is that they know I'm only here on a temporary—" She stopped herself, annoyed that she'd been about to give away too much. The client couldn't know she had a finite agreement with the firm. "I'm here part-time. They all know that, right?"

Karen reluctantly nodded. "It doesn't matter."

"But it's not as if I stole anyone's account."

"There are a lot of associates who used to work on the Decker account. They're sure they'll be the first to go."

"Right." Mia drummed her fingers. "Once we have a handle on how the foundation should be administered," she said, waving at the stack of contracts, "we'll need a lot more help. I'm sure Stan Peabody did his best, but we both know he was in way over his head. I don't know, maybe you could kind of hint around that we'll be building a team—"

"It's not just—" Karen pressed her lips together and stared at the floor.

"What?"

"Landing an account like this is great, okay? Everyone is pleased, but they aren't fooled. Unless we land a couple more of these babies, or some rich schmuck is arrested as a serial killer and hires us, there are going to be layoffs. The writing's on the wall. And no one will forget that after quitting, you came back at the worst possible time and were only hired because of David."

Mia ignored the sudden cramp in her stomach. "David? What does he have to do with—?"

"Come on, Mia. You asked. I don't know how to sugarcoat it for you." Karen didn't seem nervous anymore, but was more agitated. "Everyone knows about the two of you."

"Really? And what do they know that I don't?"

Karen's eyebrows rose. "Didn't you go on vacation together?"

"No," Mia said coolly. "I went to Hawaii with my two college friends, my business partners. As a matter of fact, we'd hoped to hook up with three guys we'd met during spring break back when we were in college."

"I'm sorry." Karen looked confused and embarrassed. Very surprised.

Mia felt only mildly bad since technically she hadn't lied. "Perhaps the rumor mill should get its facts straight."

"I'm sorry," Karen said again. "I didn't participate in the gossip, but I have to admit I made the same assumption, with you both coming in tan and the way David's been looking at you…" She trailed off, clearly miserable and disgusted with herself.

"How has David been looking at me?"

Karen got to her feet. "I think I've done enough damage."

Mia clamped her mouth shut. The smart, dignified thing to do would be to let Karen go, leave the conversation as it stood, resting firmly on Mia's denial. Even though the veteran attorney wasn't normally a talker, maybe with a few well-chosen words she'd quiet the troublemakers about their suspicions.

"Karen?" Mia swallowed—hard—and she hoped it wasn't her pride that just plummeted to the pit of her stomach. "About David—" Oh, God, she really needed to shut up. "I have to know."

THE MEETING WITH HIS UNCLE and Peter ended, and David left Harrison's corner office just as Karen Flint left Mia's. He'd been avoiding Mia all morning, and if she'd noticed, he assumed she knew the reason. Or perhaps not. She was still angry with him despite the noble gesture of tearing up the contract and adamantly declining a raise.

She had no idea how much that display of concern had touched him, though he wasn't surprised. That's the kind of person Mia was in every respect. How easy it could have been for her to hide behind her anger and pain, and abuse the power she had over the firm. She was acutely aware of how much they needed her.

A lump rose in his throat just thinking about the incident. Hell, this was precisely why he had to stay away from her. Hiding his feelings for her wasn't easy anymore. Even though he knew damn well she wasn't convinced that his motive for following her to Hawaii had been pure. Sure, he sometimes got hot under the collar when she treated him as if he were a snake, but when he was in a more reasonable mood he understood she needed time.

And he needed to keep his distance.

He decided he'd been standing idly in the hall like an idiot long enough, and took a deep breath, knowing he'd have to pass her office on his way to the reception desk. Focusing on the large envelope he needed to deliver to Laura for courier pickup, he took long purposeful strides. He'd almost made it past Mia's office when out of the corner of his eye he thought he saw her packing a box.

He backed up, ducked his head in and watched her pick up a stack of file folders and drop them into the small cardboard box. "Mia, how's it going?" he asked casually, his heart damn near beating out of his chest. Had she changed her mind? Was she calling it quits?

She looked up. "I was going to phone you," she said, averting her gaze.

"I have a few minutes now." He glanced at the envelope—the courier would be stopping at reception in the next fifteen minutes—then he noticed a paralegal walk out of the next office. "Tara," he called, "mind dropping this off at reception for me?"

"No problem, Mr. Pearson." She hurried toward him and accepted the envelope, her prying eyes darting to Mia before giving him a smile and heading toward the front.

He slipped into Mia's office, his hand on the doorknob. "Open or closed?"

She moved an indifferent shoulder, and flatly watched him close the door before shifting her gaze back to her task.

In the tense quiet, he watched her set the last folder in the box, and figured the only reason he hadn't busted a blood vessel yet was because this was the calmest he'd seen her since he'd made the offer. Perhaps too calm. Maybe she'd come to a decision. About them.

Uneasiness churned in his stomach. "You should've seen Harrison's face when I gave him the check."

"I'm glad it can help," she said, distractedly.

"What are you doing, Mia?"

She looked up then, stared blankly at him and then down at the box. "I know this is presumptuous, but it dawned on me that I can handle most of this paperwork at home."

"I'm sure you'll understand why I prefer you take copies and not originals," he said, while he searched for a tactful way to find out what was wrong. Then it occurred to him what he'd just said. His admonishment wasn't simply unnecessary, it was insulting.

"These are copies." She closed the box, showing no sign of taking offense, which was disturbing in and of itself.

"I'm sure," he muttered. "Have I told you how much I appreciate what you're doing for us?"

She blinked, refusing to look up. "Several times," she said tightly. "No need to repeat it."

That she would be impervious to his thoughtlessness but annoyed at his gratitude sent a shaft of apprehension down his spine. He'd said nothing to her since yesterday, and he was quite clear that their limited contact was to her liking. So what had her suddenly packing up her work and avoiding his gaze? "Is there a problem I should be aware of?" he asked cautiously. "With Karen, perhaps?"

"No." Mia shook her head. "No. Karen's great. She should take over the account when I leave."

He should relish the thought of her eventually leaving for good because it would make everything simpler for them. But he faced the notion with certain dread.

At least now he got to see her, and if even for a second, lose himself in her beautiful green eyes. "Is this about us?"

She met his gaze, hers filled with so much confusion and anger and sadness it practically cut him in half. "David, there is no us."

MIA SAT IN THE OFFICE of Anything Goes, doing paperwork while waiting on a shipment of smartphones and BlackBerrys. With Shelby and Lindsey at the warehouse taking a final inventory before opening day tomorrow, it was quiet and the perfect time for Mia to get a chunk of work done. If only she could shut off the incessant background noise in her helpless brain.

She wished she hadn't seen with her own eyes the proof of the firm's downward spiral. In one way, it softened her to David's dilemma, but at the same time, convinced her that he would've done anything to get her back in order to buy the firm some time to recover.

Her talk with Karen last week hadn't helped. Every instinct had told Mia to leave it alone, to refrain from urging Karen to spill what was being said about Mia and David. But no, Mia had to open Pandora's box. How could she have been so dense that she didn't know people had been talking about them? Not everyone but enough of the staff. And not just since she'd returned to the firm, but for a whole year.

Cracks had been made about the many nights they'd worked late together, about how the emotionless David, man of stone, undressed her with his eyes, how she'd gazed longingly at him from afar. Stupid high school bullshit that had made her sick.

A paralegal, whom Mia knew and liked, had actually

instigated three different office pools wagering on when they'd have their first date, at what point they'd screw each other's brains out and finally, whether and when they'd announce a wedding date. It was all so humiliating, especially considering how much Mia had prided herself in being circumspect about her feelings for David. And him…oh, God, he would be mortified to hear a quarter of the gossip that had circulated.

He wouldn't ever know, of course. At least not from her. She'd spare him that, just like she was pretty sure Karen had spared her some of the details.

It wasn't fair being the topic of break-room gossip. They'd both worked damn hard and had the track records to prove it. And this was their legacy?

To top things off, now the stupid creeps were all pissed because they thought she was getting a free ride at their expense. Screw them. She was helping to save their damn jobs. But she couldn't say anything. Not even to Karen. Mia had given David her word.

What got to her the most was all that wasted time. She and David had been tap dancing around each other for nothing, and now their relationship had come down to this sad, confusing end. She was mad at him, too, damn it, for bottling up his feelings and not saying something sooner. Of course she hadn't, either, but she'd been serious about her career, and if she'd opened up and been wrong, where would that have left her?

Oh, God, it was her fault, too. She knew that. It was all such a nightmare, she wasn't thinking straight.

And yet, she still thought about him. All the time. Even though she'd been working from home for a week, balancing her responsibility toward Anything Goes and the firm and strategically planning her required trips to the office to meet with Karen. Twice she'd made the dreaded trek, timing it so she didn't have to bump into David. It was bad enough that it was impossible to avoid other employees, but Karen sympathetically met with her in the conference room on the floor below, where Mia didn't know all of the assistants and paralegals.

Sometimes when she was alone like this, with no distractions, her thoughts strayed back to the time they'd spent in Hawaii and how simple being together had seemed. It made her smile a little, but inevitably, the longer she thought about him, the more the resentment mounted. Which in turn angered her because she had no business wasting her precious energy when it was needed for Anything Goes. Although she hadn't burdened them with her trouble, she knew she was doing Lindsey and Shelby a huge disservice.

Someone opened the front door. She pasted on a smile for the delivery man before she looked up. Except it wasn't him.

Annabelle, looking sharp in a deep red outfit that matched her hat and showed off her white hair, strode into the office.

Mia jumped out of her chair. "Annabelle, I've missed you! You've been gone so long? I left messages."

"I know, dear, I just arrived today." The woman laughed when Mia hugged her as tightly as she could. "I came as soon as I listened to your message. What on earth is going on?"

"So much. I did it. I left the firm," Mia said, and then dissolved into tears.

16

Annabelle held Mia away from her to look at her. "What's wrong?"

Embarrassed, Mia waved a hand and used her other to dab fiercely at her cheeks. "Nothing. I'm tired and being stupid and— Oh, my God, Annabelle, so much has happened since you've been away."

"Apparently." She smoothed back Mia's hair, and urged her to sit down, before situating herself on the upholstered guest chair. "Tell me everything."

"I told you I wanted to stop practicing law, remember?" she said, trying gracefully to wipe away the last of her humiliating tears. "You know I was thinking about starting a concierge business. Shelby, Lindsey and I jumped in. I can't wait for you to meet them."

Her brows still puckered, Annabelle's anxious gaze rested on Mia's face. "You look terrible despite the color in your cheeks."

"Oh, I went to Hawaii for a week. See, I told you a lot's happened." Thinking about Hawaii naturally made her think of David, and she had to blink to keep the tears from welling again.

"Mia." Annabelle took her clammy hand and sandwiched it between her much smaller palms. "Now tell me the rest."

And Mia did. Almost everything. About how David had followed her to Hawaii, how happy she'd been until she found out the firm wanted her back, apparently at any cost. How she couldn't completely trust that David hadn't come after her for personal gain. As miserable as she was, she managed not to betray the firm's confidentiality, saying only that there was a good reason why she couldn't tell anyone why she had returned. She faltered when she got to the part about how people had been talking behind their backs, and she had to pause for a deep, calming breath for fear there'd be more tears.

"It's awful to be in that place," she said. "I hate the looks I get. I hate that David doesn't know about those bast—busybodies, but I would never tell him, either. I'm pretty mad at him, but not that mad."

Annabelle's concerned eyes narrowed slightly. "Why are you angry with David?"

Mia gave an inelegant snort. Didn't anyone listen to her anymore? "Because I can't be sure that he didn't come to Hawaii just to hire me back."

"Hmm, I see. You don't trust him."

Mia stiffened. "Of course I trust him."

Annabelle, her preoccupied gaze darting out the window, said, "You'd better think about that one, dear."

Mia was feeling edgy and defensive suddenly. "What I mean is, I trust him in every other way. He's loyal to the firm and his family, to a fault, in my opinion. Definitely to his clients, too."

"So he hasn't changed his colors, per se."

Mia rubbed her forehead. Annabelle was giving her

a headache. "No, David is an honorable man. It's one of the qualities I love—" She cleared her throat. "I admire him. I'm sure he didn't want to have to trick me into going back to the firm, but he'd been backed against the wall."

Annabelle's expression grew a bit alarmed, and she fidgeted with the big, gaudy rhinestone ring she seemed to favor. "Why are you so sure he tricked you?"

"I'm not. But if you could see how dismal it is around the office— People are really scared." She shook her head. "The tension was so thick I could barely breathe."

"Imagine what it must be like for David," Annabelle said quietly, and Mia briefly closed her eyes as cold dread washed over her. "If he's the man you say he is, he would feel responsible for the well-being of those frightened people."

Mia's mouth had grown unbearably dry. "He absolutely feels that way. I know him."

Annabelle smiled a little, but she seemed clearly distracted.

"Is something wrong, Annabelle?" Mia asked, ashamed that she'd been so absorbed with her own problems that she hadn't noticed the strain on the woman's face.

"What? Oh, I'm just—" She shook her head.

Mia hesitated, unsure how hard to push. She was distracted as well.

Annabelle's remark about Mia not trusting David wouldn't leave her be. The lawyer in her fully understood the impossible task with which David had been presented. It was the woman in her who couldn't stop wondering if she'd been the sacrifice.

"You asked me once if I had any children," Annabelle said. "And I told you it hadn't been in the cards. There was a bit more to it than that. My Broadway career was more important to me than marriage and having children. You see, back then women had fewer choices. I knew I could continue to dance and act into my forties if I weren't encumbered by children, and my Herman, rest his soul, tried to convince me that he would never stand in my way, even if we were married."

The sadness in Annabelle's eyes was so real it hurt to look at her. "I didn't believe him. Bless him, he waited for me anyway. We didn't marry until I was fifty. No child-bearing years left, but we were happy for eight wonderful years." She gave a small, sad shrug. "Herman was ten years my senior. A heart attack took him in his sleep."

Mia gasped softly. "Only eight years. I'm so sorry."

Emotions clouded the older woman's eyes. "I have regretted the decision not to marry him earlier every single day. He left me a very wealthy woman, and once in a while," she said, fondly squeezing Mia's hand, "a ray of sunshine enters my life. But nothing changes the fact that I was a very foolish, self-absorbed young woman who couldn't see past her nose."

Mia sighed. "Like me?"

"Only you can answer that." Annabelle smiled. "You have a fine logical mind, something being a lawyer requires, I'd imagine. And sometimes, I'd wager you ignore logic and go with your gut. This time, Mia, what does your heart say?"

Mia's eyes blurred and she had to put a hand on the counter to steady herself. She said she'd trusted him, but that hadn't been true at all.

How would she have reacted if David had turned his back on his family firm and all the employees? She would've been horrified and convinced he wasn't the man she thought he was. She also would've been crushed that he hadn't offered her the chance to help.

He'd been pounded into a corner, and it was his honor that that kept him there. He was in hell, facing those employees every single day and unable to say a word. She'd hardly been able to handle the heat for two lousy days herself.

God, he'd practically begged her to trust him, to believe that he was still the man he'd been in Hawaii. She moaned as her body rocked with how stupid she'd been. The damn fool loved her, and instead of being a comfort, she'd made him the enemy. Why hadn't he…? No. She knew exactly why he hadn't told her he loved her. Because she hadn't trusted him.

It was probably far too late, but she had to make this right. Tell him she loved him, admit that she'd been a fool, that she'd been the one who couldn't be trusted. It would kill her to be so near him once he knew the truth, but she would suck it up and go back to work because she owed him that much. More. If by some miracle, he still loved her too, then she would fight.

Damn the delivery guy for being late. She needed to see David, the sooner the better. But she couldn't just leave the office. She jumped a bit as she realized Annabelle was still there. "Oh, God. I'm such an idiot."

Annabelle's troubled eyes looked suspiciously damp. "No, you're not the idiot. I'm afraid I am—

Mia abruptly stood. "I have a huge favor to ask you."

"Yes? Anything."

"I'm expecting a shipment at any minute." She sniffled. "But I have to see David. Now. It can't wait. I do love him, Annabelle. With all my heart—"

"Go." Annabelle spryly sprang up from her chair. "Don't you worry about a thing. Go," she repeated, practically shoving Mia toward the door. "And when you return, we need to talk. There's something very important that I must tell you."

"We will talk. I promise. And thank you." She kissed the woman's cheek. "I'll be back as soon as I can."

The door opened. They both turned, expecting the delivery guy.

David tentatively crossed the threshold.

"David? What are you doing here?"

His smile was faint as he glanced from Mia to Annabelle, back to Mia. "I have to talk to you. It's personal."

"I was just coming to talk to you," Mia said, her heart warming when she touched his arm and hope entered his eyes.

"Good," Annabelle said, startling David. "You two, skedaddle. Right now."

Mia laughed nervously as Annabelle pretty much steamrolled them out the door and onto the sidewalk.

David looked as if he didn't know what to think.

"I'll wait for Lindsey and Shelby," Annabelle said, her trembling hand pressed to her stomach. "Don't hurry back. Now get."

THEY WENT TO Mia's loft since it was close. The place was messy because, with three women and too much stuff, they hadn't fallen into a satisfactory routine yet.

Mia didn't care. She shoved aside a heap of freshly

washed towels and made room for both of them on the couch. She sat first, in the middle, forcing him to sit close. He didn't seem to mind, and made no effort to move when their knees touched.

"Ah, Mia, I have so much to—"

"No," she said, holding up a hand. "Let me talk first."

His watchful eyes narrowed slightly, but he gestured for her to go on.

"I'm not staying with the firm."

He didn't seem surprised or even upset. Disappointment did flicker in his eyes because, to his credit and to her relief, he did nothing to keep his feelings in check. Still, he only nodded.

"That's not to say I'm bailing on you. I'm not. I'll stay on, but only as a consultant." She paused, and found she didn't have to dig for courage. This was so right that it had to be said. "I admire you, David, your loyalty, your sense of responsibility. It's all part of who you are, and I love that about you. I love you. And we deserve a chance." She'd hardly dared to breathe, and it all came out in a whoosh. "I'm sorry I didn't trust you enough, but I do love you, and I hope we still have a chance to make things work."

David blinked, and then took his time studying her. "A consultant, huh? I came up with a similar solution, although I do like mine better."

She didn't say a word, just waited for him to continue, her heart beating faster and faster. He could've said he loved her, too. Was she wrong? No, not about David. She'd been confused for a while, but never wrong. He'd always been the man she thought him to be. The man she wanted.

"Yes, of course, for obvious reasons I would like it if you stayed with the firm. But if that doesn't work out, and I have to knock on every door in Manhattan to find another client, so be it. I won't let you go. I love you, too, Mia. I have for a long time. And I promise you I will never let anything come between us again." He took her hand, kissed it.

"Oh, David." Her voice broke. "I've loved you for a long time, too."

A reluctant smile tugged at his mouth. "I guess everyone knew but us."

The office gossip. Oh, God. He had to be mortified. "You know?"

He sighed. "I know. Maybe it's not too late to make my bet in the office pool," he said dryly, and Mia laughed in spite of herself. "We could make a killing." He reached into his pocket and pulled out a small jeweler's box. "Insider trading be damned."

Her heart nearly jumped out of her chest.

"I don't want you just to be part of the firm. Be part of the family, Mia. Be my wife." He opened the blue velvet box. "Marry me."

She started breathlessly at the beautiful sparkling diamond…a princess cut, at least two carats. "You aren't even drawing a salary."

David laughed. "Not the answer I was hoping for."

Mia threw her arms around him. The tears already filling her eyes. "Yes." Her voice broke. "Yes," she said more strongly. "Yes."

He buried his face in her hair, his arms tightly around her, and she felt the shudder go through his body. "I love you so much," he whispered, his voice a low, throaty murmur.

She was the one who finally drew back. She wanted to look at him, wanted him to kiss her. He took her face in his hands, and she threaded her hands through his hair. Then he pressed his firm, reassuring lips to her trembling mouth.

TWO HOURS HAD PASSED before they headed to Anything Goes. Mia hoped Lindsey and Shelby had relieved Annabelle. Although Mia knew without a single doubt that Annabelle would have no problem having been stuck there, especially once she saw the ring.

Before Mia opened the door she heard the laughter and excited chatter. Annabelle sat at the desk, Shelby was perched on the counter and Lindsey sat in the guest chair. They all turned to look at David and Mia. While her two partners grinned in unison, Annabelle looked a bit anxious.

"Well?" Shelby said. "Have you two kissed and made up?"

"Pretty much," Mia said, casually flipping back her hair making sure the rock on her finger caught the light.

Annabelle's eyes sparkled as brilliantly as the diamond. Covering her mouth with her blue-veined hand, she leaped up from the chair and fiercely hugged Mia. "I'm so relieved."

Laughing, Mia hugged the woman back.

Lindsey gasped, her hand going to her throat.

"Am I missing something?" Shelby frowned, then her eyes widened the second she spotted the ring. "Holy crap."

"Yes, indeed," Annabelle said, let Mia go and turned

to David. "I'm so happy to finally meet you, young man. "I've heard many fine things about you."

"Pleased to meet you." He extended Annabelle his hand, which she ignored, and hugged him as tightly as she'd hugged Mia.

David flushed a bit and helplessly patted the older woman's back.

Mia laughed. "I'm sorry we were gone so long. We had a lot to sort out."

Shelby had grabbed her hand and was studying the ring. "No problem. Annabelle gave us some terrific ideas, like shopping estate sales for inventory." She passed Mia's hand to Lindsey. "Good job, Pearson. You have any brothers?"

"Sorry."

"Oh, well." Shelby shrugged. "Hey, Linds, I'll flip you for Mia's room."

Lindsey rolled her eyes, and hugged Mia. I'm so happy for you, sweetie." She smiled at David. "You did good."

"I think so," he said, slipping an arm around Mia's waist.

Mia met his eyes. It didn't seem totally real yet. David. Them. She stole another glance at the ring. "Hey I'm not giving up my share of the loft quite yet, guys. Looks as if I'll have to put in more time at the firm."

"That won't be necessary," Annabelle said quietly. "Unless you want to, of course. Though certainly not on my account." She dabbed at a tear that slid down her cheek. "I am so sorry, Mia. I thought I was helping. But it seems I'm simply a foolish old woman who needs to keep her nose out of everyone's business."

Seeing that Annabelle was visibly shaken, Mia took

her friend's ice-cold hand. "Annabelle, whatever it is, it's okay."

She shifted, dabbed again at her cheek. "My apology extends to you as well, David. I hope you both can eventually forgive me."

He stared at Annabelle, his expression one of graduating awareness. "Stan Peabody?"

"A very old and dear friend," Annabelle said. "He's managed my affairs for too long. He needs to retire. If you aren't totally disgusted with me, I'd like Pearson and Stern to take over the entire estate. My late husband... he had a knack for making money."

Mia let out a short, self-deprecating laugh. Talk about self-absorbed. Her friend had given her hint earlier, but Mia had failed to connect the dots. "Why, Annabelle? Why the charade?"

She sighed. "The last time we were in the park, you sounded so miserable, and I honestly didn't believe you wanted to leave your job. I thought if I could somehow force you two together, you would stop thinking about running away from David, and he would see what a wonderful young woman you are." She cast an apologetic look at Lindsey and Shelby. "I'm afraid I didn't realize how serious you were about your business venture. And then I left on my cruise. You quit the firm, and I very nearly made a mess of everything." Her damp eyes lighting with hope, she glanced from Mia to David. "However, I dare say, it seems to have worked out."

After a brief, stunned silence, Mia gave her a mock glare. "You obviously have too much time on your hands, young lady."

"Not anymore." With hands on her hips, Lindsey snagged Annabelle's gaze. "You have some outstanding ideas, and Shelby and I shamelessly plan to keep picking your brain."

Annabelle sighed, her face looming with relief. "There's a nice, cozy little bar not far from here. I'm buying."

"I'm in." Shelby looped an arm with Annabelle and, winking at Mia, she said, "You two don't wait up."

They stopped at the door long enough for Annabelle to give Mia and David a final beatific smile. "I assume you understand that Pearson and Stern will have all of my business. I'll have Stan fill you in on the rest of it tomorrow."

Wordlessly, they watched the three of them leave the office.

"The rest of it? Mia said.

"That's what I heard." David pulled her into his arms, and she linked her hands around his neck,

"I wasn't about to ask." Mia's heart fluttered at the way the love shone in his warm brown eyes. "I wish we were in Hawaii right now."

"Hawaii was great, but it doesn't matter where we are." He kissed her gently. "As long as we're together."

She nodded. "Oh, God, they're all going to have a field day at the office when they find out."

"Don't care."

Mia smiled. "You've come a long way."

"Yes, I have," He kissed her hair, her eyelids, her mouth. "My place?"

"Definitely." Mia didn't even mind when he started kissing her, and it was another hour before they closed the office door behind them.

* * * * *

COMING NEXT MONTH

Available April 26, 2011

#609 DELICIOUS DO-OVER
Spring Break
Debbi Rawlins

#610 HIGH STAKES SEDUCTION
Uniformly Hot!
Lori Wilde

#611 JUST SURRENDER...
Harts of Texas
Kathleen O'Reilly

#612 JUST FOR THE NIGHT
24 Hours: Blackout
Tawny Weber

#613 TRUTH AND DARE
Candace Havens

#614 BREATHLESS DESCENT
Texas Hotzone
Lisa Renee Jones

You can find more information on upcoming
Harlequin® titles, free excerpts and more at
www.HarlequinInsideRomance.com.

REQUEST YOUR FREE BOOKS!
2 FREE NOVELS PLUS 2 FREE GIFTS!

❦ Harlequin®
Blaze™

red-hot reads!

YES! Please send me 2 FREE Harlequin® Blaze® novels and my 2 FREE gifts (gifts are worth about $10). After receiving them, if I don't wish to receive any more books, I can return the shipping statement marked "cancel." If I don't cancel, I will receive 6 brand-new novels every month and be billed just $4.24 per book in the U.S. or $4.71 per book in Canada. That's a saving of at least 15% off the cover price. It's quite a bargain. Shipping and handling is just 50¢ per book in the U.S. and 75¢ per book in Canada.* I understand that accepting the 2 free books and gifts places me under no obligation to buy anything. I can always return a shipment and cancel at any time. Even if I never buy another book, the two free books and gifts are mine to keep forever.

151/351 HDN FC4T

Name _____ (PLEASE PRINT) _____

Address _____ Apt. # _____

City _____ State/Prov. _____ Zip/Postal Code _____

Signature (if under 18, a parent or guardian must sign)

Mail to the **Reader Service:**
IN U.S.A.: P.O. Box 1867, Buffalo, NY 14240-1867
IN CANADA: P.O. Box 609, Fort Erie, Ontario L2A 5X3

Not valid for current subscribers to Harlequin Blaze books.

Want to try two free books from another line?
Call 1-800-873-8635 or visit www.ReaderService.com.

* Terms and prices subject to change without notice. Prices do not include applicable taxes. Sales tax applicable in N.Y. Canadian residents will be charged applicable taxes. Offer not valid in Quebec. This offer is limited to one order per household. All orders subject to credit approval. Credit or debit balances in a customer's account(s) may be offset by any other outstanding balance owed by or to the customer. Please allow 4 to 6 weeks for delivery. Offer available while quantities last.

Your Privacy—The Reader Service is committed to protecting your privacy. Our Privacy Policy is available online at www.ReaderService.com or upon request from the Reader Service.

We make a portion of our mailing list available to reputable third parties that offer products we believe may interest you. If you prefer that we not exchange your name with third parties, or if you wish to clarify or modify your communication preferences, please visit us at www.ReaderService.com/consumerschoice or write to us at Reader Service Preference Service, P.O. Box 9062, Buffalo, NY 14269. Include your complete name and address.

HBI1

*With an evil force hell-bent on destruction,
two enemies must unite to find a truth that turns
all-too-personal when passions collide.*

*Enjoy a sneak peek in Jenna Kernan's next installment
in her original* TRACKER *series, GHOST STALKER,
available in May, only from Harlequin Nocturne.*

"Who are you?" he snarled.

Jessie lifted her chin. "Your better."

His smile was cold. "Such arrogance could only come from a Niyanoka."

She nodded. "Why are you here?"

"I don't know." He glanced about her room. "I asked the birds to take me to a healer."

"And they have done so. Is that *all* you asked?"

"No. To lead them away from my friends." His eyes fluttered and she saw them roll over white.

Jessie straightened, preparing to flee, but he roused himself and mastered the momentary weakness. His eyes snapped open, locking on her.

Her heart hammered as she inched back.

"Lead who away?" she whispered, suddenly afraid of the answer.

"The ghosts. Nagi sent them to attack me so I would bring them to her."

The wolf must be deranged because Nagi did not send ghosts to attack living creatures. He captured the evil ones after their death if they refused to walk the Way of Souls, forcing them to face judgment.

"Her? The healer you seek is also female?"

"Michaela. She's Niyanoka, like you. The last Seer of Souls and Nagi wants her dead."

Jessie fell back to her seat on the carpet as the possibility of this ricocheted in her brain. Could it be true?

"Why should I believe you?" But she knew why. His black aura, the part that said he had been touched by death. Only a ghost could do that. But it made no sense.

Why would Nagi hunt one of her people and why would a Skinwalker want to protect her? She had been trained from birth to hate the Skinwalkers, to consider them a threat.

His intent blue eyes pinned her. Jessie felt her mouth go dry as she considered the impossible. Could the trickster be speaking the truth? Great Mystery, what evil was this?

She stared in astonishment. There was only one way to find her answers. But she had never even met a Skinwalker before and so did not even know if they dreamed.

But if he dreamed, she would have her chance to learn the truth.

*Look for GHOST STALKER by Jenna Kernan,
available May only from Harlequin Nocturne,
wherever books and ebooks are sold.*

Harlequin *Desire*

ALWAYS POWERFUL, PASSIONATE AND PROVOCATIVE.

USA TODAY BESTSELLING AUTHOR

MAUREEN CHILD

BRINGS YOU ANOTHER PASSIONATE TALE

KINGS *of* CALIFORNIA

KING'S MILLION-DOLLAR SECRET

Rafe King was labeled as the King who didn't know
how to love. And even he believed it. That is, until
the day he met Katie Charles. The one woman who
shows him taking chances in life can reap the best
rewards. Even when the odds are stacked against you.

Available May, wherever books are sold.

SD73096

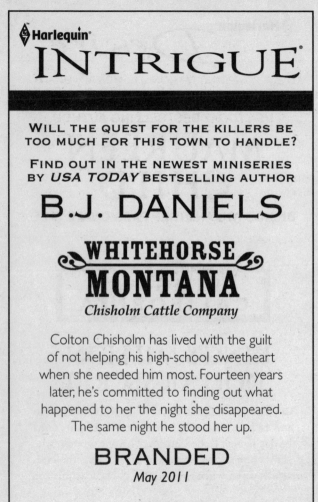